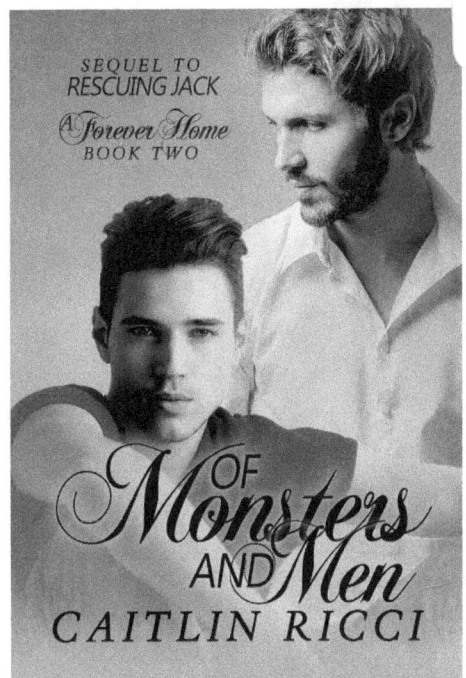

SEQUEL TO
RESCUING JACK

A Forever Home
BOOK TWO

OF
Monsters
AND *Men*

CAITLIN RICCI

"I would definitely recommend this novel to others… not only because of the rarity in finding a romance novel with an ace main character, but also to show romance readers that love really does come in all forms!"

—Just Love — Romance by Any Definition

"This was a unique read for me…"

—Prism Book Alliance

"The story ended far too soon."

—Sinfully… Addicted to All Male Romance

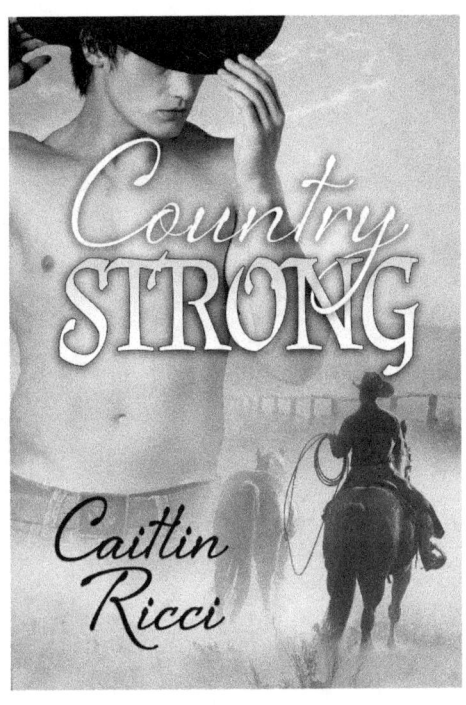

"Caitlin Ricci knows how to craft characters that seem to leap from the pages of the book. There is an honesty to the storytelling that makes the writing seem less like a fiction…"
—Sensual Reads

"*Country Strong* is a very beautiful story… would love to see this develop into a series. It has such great promise!"
—MM Good Book Reviews

"I can tell that Caitlin Ricci must be an animal lover, it was definitely written with a lot of love and affinity for pets."
—Hearts on Fire

"Thank you, Caitlin, for a beautiful story of pain, fear, terror, drama, hope, love, family, and the love of a dog."
—Rainbow Book Reviews

"I know I will be reading the next books in the series, and I highly recommend this one. I believe Caitlin Ricci has the beginnings of a wonderful series here."
—The Novel Approach

By CAITLIN RICCI

Country Strong
Cuddling (Dreamspinner Anthology)
His Lion Tamer
Marked by Grief
To the Highest Bidder

A FOREVER HOME
Rescuing Jack
Of Monsters and Men

Published by Harmony Ink Press
First Time for Everything (Harmony Ink Anthology)
Weathering the Storm

Published by DREAMSPINNER PRESS
http://www.dreamspinnerpress.com

TO THE HIGHEST BIDDER

CAITLIN RICCI

DREAMSPINNER PRESS

Published by
DREAMSPINNER PRESS

5032 Capital Circle SW, Suite 2, PMB# 279, Tallahassee, FL 32305-7886 USA
http://www.dreamspinnerpress.com/

To the Highest Bidder
© 2015 Caitlin Ricci.

Cover Art
© 2015 Caitlin Ricci.
Cover content is for illustrative purposes only and any person depicted on the cover is a model.

ISBN: 978-1-63476-141-3
Digital ISBN: 978-1-63476-142-0
Library of Congress Control Number: 2015905846
First Edition July 2015

Printed in the United States of America
∞
This paper meets the requirements of
ANSI/NISO Z39.48-1992 (Permanence of Paper).

CHAPTER ONE

I GLANCED up from the holoscreen I held as the warning indicator flashed high on the wall across from me. The blinking red light continued for a few minutes as the shuttle docked and the air lock closed outside the apartment I shared with my brother. There was a less direct way of getting home, by docking at the actual station port a few levels up, but for a shuttle as small as his, he could hook up right outside the living room and come right in. Not everyone in the station had an apartment that backed to space, but Corbin liked the convenience of simply being able to dock and then being home. And he paid the bills so I went with it. As the light switched off, the front door slid open and the automatic doorbell rang, along with a loud mechanical voice announcing my brother's return home.

"Hey," I called, moving my sore muscles enough to force myself to sit up on the couch I'd been lying on most of the afternoon while I read. The holoscreen slowly went dim from my inattention as my brother locked the automatic door behind him.

"Damn, I'm exhausted," Corbin said, plunking down on the couch beside me. Though my brother made the claim, he certainly didn't look it. Two weeks away appeared to have done well for him. His purple skin shone with a faint gold undertone, and his eyes had a sheen that had not been there when I'd last seen him.

"Business was good?" I asked, even though I was already guessing the answer from my brother's easy, definitely satisfied grin.

1

He ruffled my short hair and leaned back, resting his head on the couch. His long black hair fell over the back of it, nearly touching the floor. He closed his eyes, and for a moment I thought he wasn't going to answer me, but then my brother dug a hand into the pocket of his loose black slacks and pulled out a clear tube of credit crystals. My eyes went wide, and I reached for the container, but Corbin quickly pulled it out of my reach.

"Uh-uh, nope. This chunk is for bills. And I worked hard for it."

Coloring deeply, I nodded. "I know you did. That's a lot, though. Even after Monroe's cut?" I couldn't believe it. I knew my brother enjoyed his work, but still, that was more than I'd seen him bring home in, well, ever really.

My brother's lids lifted, revealing eyes darker than the space that lay outside our station's protective outer core. "Yeah. Monroe only takes 15 percent. And I had some great businessmen as customers this time, making a stop between planets. Wish draws all kinds, but these men were loaded. Great tippers, and my time with them wasn't half bad."

"Were they like us?" I asked eagerly, hoping to hear of these travelers who were so far outside what I knew of the world, which largely consisted of the men and women of the space station we lived on since I hardly ever got to venture off it. There was no need when everything was so conveniently brought to us. Besides, shuttle travel was expensive, and there was no reason to waste fuel.

"'Like us,' meaning Sythe?" Corbin replied, getting up and stretching his arms over his head. I nodded. "Nah, they weren't. Denobelas, the lot of them. Same as Monroe."

I sat back and said, "Oh," like I understood, even though I really didn't. I didn't know any Denobelas and had only ever seen the dominant race in hologram broadcasts. I knew they looked like the ancient race of humans that had long ago been bred out. But as Corbin had explained to me where his information holograms left off, they had their differences as well. He said it was supposedly more psychological than physical, whatever that was supposed to

2

mean. I didn't really know what he was talking about a lot of the time when he went on about the different people he met or where he went while he was working. It all sounded so fantastic to me, this whole universe I'd barely experienced but had been hearing about for years.

"What's this?" he asked.

I was about to question what he was talking about when the message started playing. I froze, sure I'd hidden it and wishing I'd done a better job of it. Corbin wasn't supposed to find out about the message, but it wasn't like I could do anything about it now.

"Congratulations, Thierry Leroux. You've been selected for the elite class of sky year 2231. You and thirty of your best and brightest peers will have the exclusive opportunity to learn from the sharpest minds of today and tomorrow at the Intergalactic Star Pilot Academy. Your acknowledgement is expected within sixty days. Here's what you'll need to bring—"

"Turn it off," I grumbled, laid my arms over my knees, then lowered my head. I didn't need to hear the message again. I'd already memorized it the first six times I'd heard it, just to be sure I knew what they were really saying. But then I'd figured out what else was on the message. Sure, my heart had soared with the possibilities of being able to be everything I'd ever wanted. Being a star pilot had been my dream since I was three and saw one of the first shuttles land on our isolated home planet. Now, nearly two decades later, I'd never forgotten about that seemingly impossible idea of being up there among the elite few.

Corbin came back to the couch and touched my shoulder. I tried to pull away, but my brother's long fingers curled in the thin material of my shirt, keeping me still. I didn't mind the restriction to my movements, but it did mean I'd have to tell Corbin, and I wasn't sure I was really able to talk about it. At least not yet.

"You've always wanted this. Why didn't you tell me you were able to get in? That's great news." The joy was obvious in his voice, but I shook my head, dismissing his words.

"I don't want it anymore. It was a stupid dream." My voice broke on the lie. Of course I still wanted it. For years I'd pictured myself in those ships, traveling the galaxy, learning everything I could about whatever they'd hand me. I wouldn't be a captain. That wasn't something I was interested in. But a pilot was a far better opportunity, especially for a poor Sythe orphan from a tiny station that was barely large enough to need a registration number.

He shook his head, released my shirt, and stepped back, giving me some room. "No, it wasn't. Why would you ever say it was?" He crouched, staring up at me with dark eyes. I didn't understand why my brother looked so hurt, so confused. Wasn't this supposed to be my life? My dream? What did it matter if I decided not to do it anymore? Was giving up really so wrong?

"I don't want it anymore," I whispered, looking away. My brother knew too much. Years as a paid aspasian for the visitors of Wish had given him too much insight into how other people worked. That he now used that ability on me, his younger brother, wasn't in the least bit fair.

He shook his head. "Yeah, you do. How about you stop lying to me, and tell me why you've decided to give up on something you've thought about for the past fifteen years?" His black brows rose unexpectedly, and I bit my lip.

It was on the tip of my tongue to lie. But as Corbin wrapped his hand around mine, and the warmth of my brother's touch fired along my sensitive nerves, I chose the better option. The truth slipped off my tongue like acid, though I knew it was the right choice. Lying to Corbin, the only family I had left in all the universe, simply wasn't an option for me.

"We can't afford it. It's too expensive."

His lips tightened, and he released me. He sat back and crossed his legs, getting comfortable on the floor in front of me. "So that's it."

I nodded, feeling lost and like I'd somehow let myself and Corbin down.

"And they don't offer scholarships for that program, do they?"

"No," I replied, though he knew that well enough. He'd sat there with me as the head of the program talked to us, walking us through the process. Orientation had lasted three straight days, and although I had loved being in the academy, I'd never thought I had the slightest chance of getting in. My test scores were fine—it wasn't that. I just didn't have the background for it. ISPA was prestigious. Always had been. They accepted and graduated only the best in the galaxy. I'd always known I didn't register anywhere near that level.

"I'll pick something else. It's fine," I told him, hoping he would let me brush off the only dream I'd ever had as easily as I'd tried to lie to him.

He snorted and shook his head. "Yeah, no, Thierry. We're not playing that game. You're going to the academy. We'll just have to find something to sell." He frowned and looked around our tiny apartment. I didn't need to look. I'd thought about that first and hadn't found anything. I'd had a full week while Corbin was away working on Wish to think of things I could sell to make the money I needed to chase that impossible dream. "Do they take payments?" he asked hopefully.

I shook my head. "Twenty thousand credits needed up front as payment, then it's five thousand every year after the first." Even talking about that much money made my stomach cramp. Corbin made a good amount in his two weeks per month serving the wealthiest of the galaxy, but he'd never brought home that much. Before I'd received the message, I hadn't ever seen that much money required for anything. Even our shuttle had cost only a fourth of that, and Corbin had been paying that off for the last five years.

Whistling low, Corbin looked as surprised as I had been. "Wow. So that's why they didn't tell us how much their academy cost when I asked. Pricey little joint, huh?" I nodded miserably. "So for three years there, you'd need thirty thousand grams of credits."

I looked at the hologram lying on the well-worn table between us. A picture of the ISPA's front door welcomed me in. If only it were that easy. I'd never wanted anything more and couldn't believe I'd been accepted; it was so far out of my reach.

"There's nothing to sell," I quietly admitted. "It's hopeless."

He was silent for several long moments, and I was sure he hadn't heard me. But then he offered an idea that was too ridiculous to be believed. "You have yourself," he said, his voice soft as I met his dark gaze.

Now it was my turn to look shocked. My mouth fell open. "You mean be a prostitute. Like you. You want me to do that?"

Corbin rolled his eyes. "Prostitute isn't what we like to be called, little brother. I am an aspasian when I'm there. It's pretty fun. And besides, it's paid your bills for the past few years, so why knock it now?"

I nodded, realizing instantly I'd crossed the line. Corbin was proud of what he did and enjoyed his work. And he was right: it had paid our bills and bought me the clothes I was wearing. If he wasn't working on Wish, we would be homeless right now, just like we had been on our home planet.

"Sorry. You're right. I…. Sorry." I felt guilty for saying what I had and for thinking badly of my brother's chosen profession. But at the back of my mind, there was some part of me that felt wrong for considering my brother's words.

"Would you leave? You know, if you could?" I asked, looking at him.

"If I could leave? You think I'm trapped there?" my brother asked, sounding at once offended and amused. I wasn't really sure what to believe anymore now that I was actually considering this. Corbin's dark lips spread into a warm smile, one he'd often claimed brought men into his bed without any further work on his part. "I wouldn't. No. Even if I found someone and fell in love with them, I wouldn't quit my job. I love it."

"You love having sex with strangers?"

Corbin snorted. "You think that's all I do? Just lie on my back and badly fake some moans?"

6

And suddenly I was bright red and stuck somewhere between complete embarrassment and curiosity. The latter won out, and I simply shrugged, unsure what else to do as my brother started talking. "People come to Asiq for the fantasy. Wish is a planet covered in brothels, but there's a big difference between Asiq and the others, and that's why I work there. They're not coming to Monroe's club for a quick lay, and his prices reflect that. We're highly valued there because we give the customers the whole package. If you wanted to do this, he'd have to train you up some, but it shouldn't be too hard. I only needed a few intense days before I was ready for my first client. We provide companionship, entertainment, and yes, when asked, we do perform sexual acts for our clients. But most of my day is not spent naked," Corbin said.

With my brother's words playing in my mind, I tried to imagine the place where my brother worked. I'd never asked, never really wanted to know what Corbin did the two weeks a month he was gone. In all honesty I'd accepted my brother's money, used it to buy food and other things we needed, but hadn't thought about it further than that. Maybe I'd been too afraid or too ashamed of what I thought my brother did for our money. Now, though, I wasn't so sure.

"Can you... um... walk me through a normal day, then?" I asked.

Corbin's brows rose. "You're really considering this, aren't you?"

"It's the only way to become a pilot, right? Smuggling would take too long. And drug running is—"

"Out of the question," Corbin snapped at me, leaning forward and catching my gaze. "Not only is that extremely dangerous, but if you're caught, there go your hopes for a future in the program anyway. So no, you're not doing that." He sighed loudly and dragged his hands through his hair. "Relax about it for now. You've got two weeks to think about what you want to do. I'll call Monroe and see what he says."

I nodded and waited as he punched buttons on the com unit attached to his wrist. "Speaker please," I whispered as he was about to put the earpiece in. Corbin complied, and a moment later the call connected.

"Miss me so soon?" an unfamiliar voice at the other end joked.

I pulled my knees up to my chest and laced my hands around my ankles. I'd never heard Monroe's voice before, but it sounded warm. What kind of man ran a brothel, especially one as successful as Asiq?

Corbin smiled. "No, old man, not yet. I've only been gone four hours. But I do have an idea for you."

"Will I like it?"

"Maybe," Corbin said, looking at me. "But right now it's only in the maybe phase. My brother had a thought."

"I'm listening."

He lifted his hand and waved me down to sit beside him. Reluctantly I went, my sore muscles from lying there too long protesting as I moved to the floor and sank onto my knees beside Corbin. "Tell him yourself," he said, his voice gentle.

"Um...." I didn't know where to begin.

"My time is valuable, Corbin, you know that. If your brother is unable to voice his needs now, perhaps you should call back later, when he is more articulate."

I swallowed thickly. I didn't know the other man at all, but I did recognize someone quickly losing their patience when I heard it. Damn. This was not how I imagined this going, not that I'd had very long to think about it before Corbin had sprung this impromptu phone call on me.

"He's thinking," Corbin quickly covered for me, but a sharp jab in my ribs told me I needed to do it much faster.

I licked my lips and leaned closer to the com unit. "Sir, I am... I'd like to.... You see...."

"Take a breath and try again," Monroe said, sounding calmer.

I tried again. "Sorry, sir. I'm a bit nervous. You see, I need to ask a favor."

There was a loud groan on the other end of the line, and I instantly felt bad for bringing it up. Of course he didn't want to hear about it. This was a stupid idea. I was an idiot for even thinking about it and wasting the other man's time.

"All right, I'm listening. You want a favor from me?"

I considered my words even as my heart raced so quickly, I thought I would pass out for sure. "I need money. Lots of it, really quickly."

Monroe chuckled. "Well, Wish is the place to make it. If you want to interview the next time your brother comes out, I'll give you one. Is that all?"

"No, you don't understand. I don't want to work for you," I quickly snapped. Then, realizing how badly that sounded, I spoke again. "I want to be a star pilot. But the academy's price tag is so far out of this galaxy, I start to feel sick just looking at it."

"So?"

I took a breath and steeled my nerves. "So I was thinking about auctioning off my virginity at Asiq." There. I'd said it. And in the silence that followed, I considered all the ways it could have gone better.

But then Monroe replied. "I would take 25 percent of the price to cover advertising and training costs."

My mouth fell open. "That's ridiculous! Corbin only gives you fifteen!"

"Yes, but your brother has been working at Asiq for years. He had a one-year contract to begin with and has extended that each year since. I've made my investment back on him. If he continues to stay, then each year after his seventh, my cut goes down until I keep just 5 percent of what he earns to cover the cost of keeping Asiq up and employing the security a place like this needs. You, on the other hand, are asking for a one-time deal. I can make it profitable for you, of that I have no doubt. Virgins are exceedingly valuable in this industry. But it will take time to train you and get the word out about what you're intending to do. So that's my offer: 25 percent."

"I don't even know if I want to do this," I grumbled, feeling foolish in light of Monroe making perfect sense. I could see the business side of things, and as little as Corbin had told me about Monroe, I at least knew he was a businessman above anything else.

"Think it over. Decide if you can handle giving yourself away to a stranger. Most people can't. I can get you the money you need for your school, but you need to decide if the price is worth it. Now, if you'll excuse me, I have some customers to take care of. Is there anything else you need, either of you?"

Corbin brought the com closer to his mouth. "No, sir. Thank you."

"And what is your brother's name?"

"Thierry," I spoke up, looking at Corbin and wishing I could give words to all the feelings swirling inside me.

"Then good-bye for now, Thierry. I'm sure we'll talk again soon."

I nodded, though Monroe couldn't see me. I'd give the man an answer either way before Corbin left again.

CHAPTER TWO

TWO WEEKS went by far too quickly, and I still didn't have an answer for Monroe. I actually half figured my brother had probably forgotten all about it in that time since neither of us mentioned it again. But as I woke up early to say good-bye to Corbin again, I knew I had to make a decision, and fast. There were too many questions, too many variables I needed to figure out, though, before I could choose a course of action and really stick with it. The letter from the academy glared at me from the holoscreen on my desk, reminding me I was quickly running out of time if I really did want to get in. There was no saving up for next year with them. If I didn't accept the position, I was done for. That was it. They didn't allow second chances. But what if I did everything Monroe said and still didn't make enough money? What then?

Could I still look myself in the mirror after selling my body?

"I'm leaving now," Corbin called from outside my bedroom door.

With a sick feeling in my gut, I opened it and looked up at my older brother, wishing Corbin could make everything right like he'd done years ago when I would have a nightmare and he'd come chase away the monsters with a song and some sweet taffy.

"What do I need to take with me?" I whispered, the words sounding choked as I forced them up and out of my throat.

Corbin looked surprised for only a moment before he quickly pushed his way into my room. My heavy duffle fell to the bed as

11

Corbin bent down and pulled a bag out of my closet. I didn't think I'd really need two bags for the trip, but I wasn't up to arguing with him either.

"Pack your shampoo, toothpaste, razors, shaving cream, soap, and enough changes of clothes to last you two weeks. Monroe has a laundry system, but you need to have options available. And take towels," Corbin said as he began tossing the clothes he knew I liked into the bag. "Don't worry about being neat right now. We need to get going. Just get it in the bag. Food isn't necessary since Monroe feeds us well, but if you have something you absolutely can't live without, take it. Just hurry. And Thierry?"

"Yeah?"

Corbin gave me a strange look before he pulled me close. "Make sure you want to do this. If we get there and you say absolutely no, then tell Monroe. This is your choice. Always your choice. You don't do anything you don't want to. Don't let the other guys mess with you, and don't take crap from anyone there. Monroe will take care of you if you can't find me. And if you decide you don't want to do this, he will find something else for you to do during the two weeks we're there. It won't be fun, but you'll probably be cleaning or helping in the kitchen. That's what he makes the guys that have bad attitudes do anyway."

I nodded and clutched Corbin's light jacket. "Thanks."

Stepping away, Corbin smirked at me. "Never thought I'd be taking you to Wish."

I blushed. "Didn't ever really plan on going."

He ruffled my short black hair. "I've got to call Monroe and let him know what you decided. Get packed. We leave in ten."

That wasn't enough time to do much of anything, but at least I'd already gotten dressed and showered early, unlike most times when Corbin left and I was barely crawling out of bed. I quickly ran around my room, grabbing everything I thought I might need and shoving it haphazardly into the bag. With seconds to spare, I was ready to go and standing in the kitchen, my knuckles turning white as I gripped the countertop.

"I don't know if I can do this," I grumbled to myself. My stomach turned, and I put a hand on it, hoping it would calm down. I hadn't been sick on our shuttle since the first time I'd been in it and did not want to meet Monroe with vomit on my breath.

Corbin came out of his room and slung his duffle over one shoulder. "Come on if you're coming," he said, his heavy boots making loud noises on the floor as he walked. I scrambled to keep up with him, not wanting to be left behind.

"I hope Monroe likes me," I said uncertainly as I mimicked Corbin's movements and put my bag over my shoulder.

Corbin chuckled and looked over at me. "You'll be fine. Remember, you're not doing this as a career. It's a one-time event for you."

"What's that mean?" I asked him. "Will I be treated differently than the other guys?"

Opening our front door and stepping out into the shiny metallic hallway of the space station, Corbin shrugged. "Some of them might. They may think you believe you're better than them. But maybe not. Asiq isn't like the other places on Wish. You don't have to hide what you are when you come back from there." He locked the door behind me, and together we made our way down the narrow space between apartments. I could hear other people moving around in their homes, but most were still asleep this early. Corbin continued talking, though his voice was a lot quieter now that we were out in the open between levels on the space station. "I work there two weeks a month, but I'm not a whore. I don't live there, and I don't take clients outside of Asiq. That's the mentality most of the guys have. We have fun when we're at work, but we don't get paid for sex the rest of the time."

"When people ask what you do, do you tell them?" I asked as we climbed a short flight of stairs to the landing bay.

Corbin shrugged. "Depends on the person. But yeah, I usually do."

"Even the guys you're with back here?" I continued. I knew my brother dated, but he'd always been pretty careful about who he brought around me. He told me where he was going, and who with, but I hadn't met someone he'd been with in at least six months.

Corbin's black brows lifted. "Especially them. But I don't usually have quickies with strangers. That's one benefit of working at Asiq. If all I wanted was sex, there are plenty of customers and guys working there that I could get sex from. That need is easily satisfied, and Monroe doesn't stand in our way if we want to have fun with each other as long as it doesn't interfere with his business. So when I meet a guy outside of work, I don't just jump into bed with him."

I nodded, getting more insight into my brother's personal life than I had in years. It wasn't that we weren't close, I just hadn't asked. I never had. Corbin had decided to apply at Asiq, and that had been the end of it. He kept his business life private and separated from the life we had at home, and I appreciated that. But I was just now realizing how much I needed to learn about what it meant to work at Asiq if I was actually going through with this.

It was an easy walk from the floor with the apartments to where the ships were kept in the shuttle bay. Our station was small, but it was one of the few places to fuel up this far away from the central planets. The shuttle bay doors opened when Corbin put his palm on the reader, and minutes later I strapped myself into the shiny black passenger pod of Corbin's shuttle. Our bags were secured in a cabinet behind me, and Corbin sat in front, the pilot I wanted to be. Except I didn't want to fly small station-to-planet shuttles. I wanted to explore universes. And no one would give that kind of clearance to just anyone. I needed an education to get to that level.

"There's a pack of sedatives in the cargo hold beside you," Corbin called back as the clamps released the bow of the shuttle.

There was jolt as our little ship was released, but it quickly smoothed out as the air lock ahead of us closed, followed by the one behind, and then Corbin was reversing our shuttle out into the little take-off area. We still weren't in open space, but it was close enough that I could see it through the thick window panels. Corbin swung us around, his movements precise and practiced after so many years of owning the ship.

"I don't need them," I replied as I folded my hands in my lap and wished I'd thought to bring a heavier jacket. I knew Corbin had on layers, and I hadn't put it together until now, when I was really shivering. I so rarely went into space I'd forgotten how cold it was away from the heated interior of the station. "Can I get some heat back here?"

A flick of a switch by my brother's side, and the cabin slowly filled with gentle warmth. It wasn't as much as I would have liked, but it was more than I'd had before. At least it was only a short ride to Wish. Any longer than that, and I would have had more time to think about what I was getting myself into.

"Nervous?" Corbin asked once we'd been cleared to leave the station. The final set of doors closed behind us, and I looked out into open space, a slow smile forming on my lips.

I nodded. "Yes. Were you? On your first time, I mean?"

"I didn't come to Asiq as a virgin, so things were different for me. But yeah, I was nervous. This profession will get you over being self-conscious really fast. And it can be exhausting, both mentally and physically. You don't get to have off days while you're there. If you do, you're taken out of the lineup and Monroe will give you something else to do or, if you don't want to do it anymore at all, he'll cash you out then and there, and you're gone. He doesn't play around with people who don't want to be in Asiq or aren't having a good day. The customers don't come to listen to our problems."

I let his words sink in and tried to think past the lump in my stomach.

Four hours later we were landing in a bright courtyard along with other shuttles. Once Corbin had turned off the engine, I unbuckled, grabbed our things, and met him at the door, eager to see a planet I'd only ever heard about. Wish was a small planet that had been terraformed into what it was now—a tropical paradise for the rich and wealthy. Although there were poorer brothels on the planet as well, most of them catered to the kind of people Corbin entertained. After Corbin had gotten the job at Asiq, we'd moved to the space station closest to it, and I'd been staring at the planet for the past few years but had never thought I'd ever actually be on it.

I was nearly bouncing on the balls of my feet as my brother opened the air lock and released the pressure in the shuttle. He was taking far too much time, and I wanted to see everything. But seeing it all meant I nearly fell on my face the moment the hatch was opened, since I wasn't paying attention to the ground below me. My brother's steady hand on my shoulder stopped me, though, and I shot him a sheepish smile as he brushed himself off and straightened his clothing. I realized quickly I was far underdressed when Corbin removed his jacket and revealed a dark blue button-up shirt neatly tucked into black trousers. I looked down at my faded slacks and worn-out tee, and frowned.

"You look really good," I said, taking Corbin's jacket as he handed it to me.

He laughed. "I'm at work from the minute I land. I am as expensive as I look, and these people know that. If anyone has an interest in me, I have a stack of holocards in my pocket with Asiq's logo and my name on them so people know where to find me."

"You've got it all figured out," I replied, feeling largely out of place surrounded by all the color and style of the planet. I hadn't been to all that many planets and certainly none of them looked like this one, with its bright sunshine that found me no matter where I went.

"Hey, Corbin!"

I stopped and turned at the unfamiliar voice. Corbin smiled and eagerly shook the hand of the man who approached us. "Mr. Saunders, good to see you again. Back from Alerium so soon?"

The portly man beamed, and his thick black mustache lifted with the gesture. I didn't recognize him or his name but figured there were plenty of people Corbin was friends with whom I didn't know. I'd never realized my brother knew a Nafsu. They were supposedly a rare species of alien with gray skin and short knobs that ran over the sides of their heads and up their arms. I'd always wondered if they were hard like bone or soft, like extra bits of tissue that had grown in strange places.

"I am. I cut it short to see you boys again." There was a wink and a leering smile, and I had the good sense to bite my tongue before I said anything embarrassing as I realized Mr. Saunders was not my brother's friend, but rather a customer.

"I'm sure we're looking forward to seeing you as well, sir," Corbin replied easily. I looked up at him, wondering if the smile was an act or if he really did want to have sex with the gray-skinned Nafsu again. Maybe he was just looking forward to his money. Corbin had certainly never been all that good a liar growing up.

"And who is this?"

I felt the man's eyes on me and held still, breath catching as I felt undressed and exposed by the other man. For the first time in my life, I knew I was being objectified, and it made me feel sick. I didn't understand how my brother put up with it.

"My little brother, Thierry," Corbin said, throwing an arm around my shoulders. "He's coming to visit for the next two weeks."

I wasn't sure what the look in the man's eyes meant, but suddenly I wished I'd never agreed to come on this trip. Still, I was there, and I couldn't exactly leave now, so I figured I might have to make the best of it. I met the man's gaze for as long as I could before dropping it in a moment of shyness and uncertainty that wasn't in any part an act. My brother might have improved by leaps and bounds in the lying department, but I hadn't, and I was afraid of saying something inappropriate that would get him in trouble.

"Hey," I managed to get out, followed by a grunt as Corbin poked in me in the side.

Mr. Saunders stepped closer to me, and I smelled meat on his breath. Meat was a rare delicacy, one I didn't get often, and the unfamiliar scent was at once both alluring and revolting; my stomach twisted at being so close to a man I was sure had already pictured me naked and under him.

"Will he be on the menu tonight, as well?" he asked Corbin, his voice dropping.

I bit my tongue, wanting to tell him I'd never be on this man's menu or anything else, because I wasn't a dish at a restaurant to be eaten and consumed, but Corbin beat me to it, saving me from what I was sure would have been a disaster if I'd actually said any of the things I was thinking out loud to this man.

"Not yet, but maybe soon. I'm taking him to talk to Monroe, and he'll decide from there."

Mr. Saunders smiled and stepped back. "Good. I look forward to seeing you both sometime. Brothers are one of the few delicacies I have not enjoyed at the same time."

I suppressed my gag as Corbin poked me again as if he was giving me a preemptive warning about screwing up.

"Of course. I'll see what Monroe can do for you. I'll be dancing tonight if you want to stop by and get a drink," Corbin said with a bright smile. He touched the man's hand, and Mr. Saunders gave him a heated look as he laced his fingers with Corbin's.

"I intend to be there. You save me a seat, Corbin. I like to sit up front."

His smile grew as Corbin pulled back. "I'll make sure of it, and there will be a bottle of the best wine in the sector waiting for you, as well."

"You know how to treat a man well, boy. No wonder you're so expensive." Mr. Saunders chuckled as he turned away, and I pursed my lips to keep from saying what I was thinking until the crowd had swallowed the gray man as easily as it had released him.

"What—"

"Not here," Corbin quickly cut me off.

I wanted to argue, but the look my brother gave me killed the words on my tongue. So instead I waited and kept my mouth shut, questions swirling in my mind until Corbin pulled me through the doors of a club and farther into the building until he pushed me into a small, dark alcove away from a barrage of faces I'd barely caught glimpses of when we'd entered.

"That is a customer," Corbin hissed under his breath. "One of the best Asiq has. You can't insult him!"

"I didn't," I grumbled, pushing away from him. I moved into the hallway where I could breathe better. There were voices nearby, so I made sure to keep mine low. "Did he really mean…. Would you?" I cringed, definitely sure I was never going to do that.

Corbin snorted and leaned against the wall across from me as he stuck his hands into his pockets. "Yeah, no. But that's my point. Even if I was never going to do that with him, I can't very well say that. Do you get it?"

I imagined that yeah, I probably did. But I didn't have to like it. "Sure," I mumbled.

"Ah. There you are."

CHAPTER THREE

I LOOKED up at the sound of the man's deep voice. The person standing next to Corbin made me shudder, and not because of fear or any other negative emotion. No, the man next to my brother was just that handsome. I knew that Denobelas were considered one of the prettier races by many of the planets, but I'd never actually seen them up close. Now that I was in this man's company, I found I couldn't look away, even if I'd wanted to.

"Monroe," Corbin said, releasing my shirt. "This is Thierry."

By his tone I knew Corbin wasn't ready to forgive me yet for screwing up. Whatever, that wasn't my focus right then. I wasn't sure what was expected of me when faced with the brothel's owner, but I managed a quick nod anyway as I felt heat rising in my cheeks.

Monroe smiled at us both and gave me an assessing once-over. Unlike with Saunders, this kind of look didn't bother me. I wasn't stupid, and I knew I was still being judged and didn't expect that to change anytime soon, at least not while I was on this planet. But Monroe's appraising look didn't make me feel like an object. Instead I almost felt… special. It took me a long moment to finally remember I needed to breathe, and when it happened, I ended up coughing as air rushed back into my lungs.

Forehead wrinkled as if he was concerned, Monroe looked away from me to address Corbin. "Is he ill?"

Corbin quickly shook his head. "I think you just startled him, is all. First time around one of you."

Monroe chuckled, and if it was possible, became even more attractive as his dark eyes appeared to sparkle. He wore black slacks, a silk shirt the color of the plums I'd only ever read about, and a black vest over it. It had shiny silver buttons I desperately wanted to touch. Did they all dress so well? It made me feel wholly out of place in Corbin's hand-me-downs. Though Corbin did well in Asiq, I knew we had more bills than credits most months, and I didn't blame my brother for my lack of new things. Still, I couldn't help the sharp jealousy that flared inside me at seeing someone not much older than Corbin wearing such fine things.

"Corbin, put your things in your room. I've given Thierry the vacant room next to yours. Your thumbprint opens both doors. Hurry, though. Your first appointment is in an hour."

Corbin looked surprised. "Who is it?"

"Mrs. Marsden," Monroe replied.

Corbin blushed faintly and left with a smile. I frowned after him, unsure what to make of his expression. Was he actually looking forward to having sex with a woman? Hadn't my brother always been gay? Did being on Wish change that about him too?

"You look confused," Monroe said, stepping up to me. I tried to fix whatever in my face had given me away with such speed. I wasn't used to being read so easily. "You've got questions, I'm sure."

I nodded. "I do. For starters—"

"We'll continue this in my office. I haven't felt the need to hide in private alcoves in nearly a decade."

Uneasiness came to life within my belly, and I hesitated as Monroe turned away. Without my brother around, I felt out of place and vulnerable on a planet where I was so sure I didn't belong.

"I'm not at all like everyone else here," I told Monroe, hoping I didn't insult the man, but still wanting to make things clear to him from the beginning. I followed him to his office.

Monroe half turned and gave me a level stare. "And yet you're here, hoping to sell what is most precious to a young person in exchange for money. You may not have the same place as the others, but none of the men in my employ are your typical whores either. That's why I don't allow them to be called such. Come along and learn if you wish. Or, if you've decided against this venture already, I'll show you to the kitchen, where you may work off your stay for the next two weeks. You'll earn a little there but not nearly what you're hoping to get. The choice is yours, Thierry, though I do hope you make it quickly. Running an exclusive and profitable company requires a good deal of my time, which you are currently wasting."

Sufficiently chided, I stepped forward. Monroe gave me a small smile before leading me down the corridor. Though I didn't see anyone else around, I certainly heard them in the rooms we passed. Low moans and the sound of someone begging for more put color in my cheeks, and I walked faster to keep up with Monroe.

"Did we come through a side door?" I asked, an idea slowly coming to me.

Monroe didn't slow as we rounded a corner. The pale green hallway we'd been in before opened into a cream one. Though the doors on either side reminded me of a hotel, the feel was decidedly different. Asiq was cleaner, more welcoming and inviting in a way the few hotels I'd been in simply weren't. We passed little alcoves with chairs, tables, and small plates filled with sweet treats, and entire rooms with walls covered in brightly colored silk.

"Do you ask because of the lack of people?" Monroe replied.

"In part," I quickly said as I stretched my legs to keep up with Monroe's long strides. "But also because I didn't see a sign when we came in or any sort of front desk. Don't people check in first or something?"

Monroe nodded and came to a quick stop at one of the doors. I had to stop short to avoid running into him. There was a plaque on the wall that declared it as the office, but otherwise the door looked like every other one along the wall. I frowned, expecting an owner to give himself more and not understanding why Monroe apparently hadn't.

Monroe placed his thumb on a small panel, and a second later, there was a low beep, followed by the audible click of the door unlocking. It swung inward, and Monroe moved with it, with me silently trailing behind.

"All our doors are thumbprint recognizing," Monroe explained as he closed the door behind me. "I'll import yours into the system as soon as we have a quick chat. Take a seat in front of the desk."

I nodded and quickly moved to do as he asked. I was conflicted as I settled into the seat. Being on Wish made my decision all the more real, and part of me wanted to run. Another smaller part thought if I annoyed Monroe enough, the man wouldn't want to help me anyway and I'd be sent away. Corbin would only know Monroe hadn't liked me, and so I could save face with my brother and get out of this situation without looking like I'd left because I was so afraid. But then I remembered why I was there and what it meant to me to be able to become a pilot. I had to do this. Yeah, it wasn't my first choice, but I didn't really have any other options. Not ones that were legal, anyway.

Monroe sat across the sleek glass desk from me and pulled out a holocard. "We'll start with the basics, and you can ask questions after I input this information. Begin with your age."

"Twenty," I answered automatically. The holocard recorded my answer.

"Any known diseases? You'll be blood-tested as well. And know, Thierry, that if you lie to me on any of these questions and I find out, you'll be banned from ever setting foot in Asiq again."

I pursed my lips and shook my head. "None." Monroe's threat didn't do a whole lot for me since, after this was done, I didn't ever plan on coming back there again.

Monroe tapped his fingers on the glass beneath his hands, and I looked around the minimally decorated office. There was a partially open door behind Monroe, and I bit my tongue at the sight of the big four-poster bed beyond it.

"Do you live here?"

Monroe briefly turned to follow my gaze. "I do. With thirty rooms available, I see no reason to keep a separate residence. None of my employees do, however. Not only would I find their constant presence here an intrusion into my life, I find that customers like being surprised by fresh faces every few weeks."

That made sense, and I was ready to dismiss that detail, but a noise from the room drew my attention there again. "Do you have a pet?"

Monroe smirked and shook his head. "It's Dion, getting dressed. Now back to your interview—"

"You have sex with the men here? Like my brother?" I asked him sharply. As Monroe's dark brows rose, I knew it had been the wrong thing to ask, and his darkening expression confirmed it.

He put the holocard away and leveled a glare at me as I began to fidget. "Do you think I force the men in my employ to have sex with me? That part of your interview will be done on your knees?" His tone was even, and I had no idea if I'd actually angered the other man or not, but I was pretty sure I had.

I shrugged. "I… I don't know. I mean, this is my first time here. And I know Corbin enjoys his work, but maybe that's because you're really good, and maybe that's how things are done on Wish, and I just don't know." My face flamed, and I bit my bottom lip to keep from saying anything more to embarrass myself. "Should I let myself out? I mean, if I really screwed this up and all, I should be going now. Right?" I started to get up, but the warmth of Monroe's hand over mine on top of the desk stopped me.

"No. Stay. This interview isn't over."

I quickly retook my seat and leaned toward Monroe, wanting to get on with it if he was going to let me continue. I wasn't eager for the sex part, but I did want out of his office. I wanted to explore and see things and know for myself I'd really made the right choice in coming there, and I wasn't going to be able to decide that while sitting at a desk.

Monroe removed his hand from mine and laid it on the table between us. "Yes, I have sex with the men in my employ. When they want to. We all have healthy sexual appetites—that's generally why we're here. I don't employ men with habits that need feeding or emotional baggage that keeps them in this line of work. Your brother, like every other man here, works because he wants to. They work for me because I'm the best. And you're right. I am that good."

I quickly looked away at the man's wink. "Uh… okay."

Monroe pulled the holocard toward him again. "What is your sexual history?"

I'd expected this kind of question but still squirmed at the idea of sharing the intimate details with another person, especially a stranger. Thankfully I didn't have all that much to disclose.

"I kissed a guy when I was thirteen."

"And?" Monroe asked, starting to sound impatient.

I shifted in the chair. "I made a guy come with my hand. Once. When I was seventeen."

Monroe nodded. "There is no physical way to check the virginity of a man, so I'll have to take your word for it. But I want you to know, if you're lying to me and this event happens anyway, I will not be happy in the least."

"Of course not," I replied, bristling at the idea of someone thinking I'd lie about that.

The smile Monroe gave me wasn't friendly in the least. "Lying isn't tolerated here. If you do, I'll not only ban you, I'll suspend your brother for six months as well."

My brows shot up, and my mouth fell open. "You can't punish Corbin!"

"I can't? I'm his employer, so yes, I can do that and so much more to him. I'm taking his word on your virginity as much as I'm taking yours. Asiq does so very well because clients know they will get the best experience here. My men aren't whores and a fantasy fulfilled here is so much more than simply sex. Virginity is a pricey commodity, and I said I could get you the money you need for your career. That isn't a problem. A cute Sythe virgin will be an easy sell. If I give my word that you're innocent, I put my reputation on the line as well. This has never been done on Wish before, though with how pricey virgins are I'm sure it will be a successful auction, and I will not have the precedent set with the failure of Asiq. Do I make myself clear?"

I sat back, feeling cold as the pressure of Monroe's words hit me hard in the chest. "I understand," I said.

Monroe nodded. "In light of the gravity of what you'll be agreeing to, is there anything else you wish to disclose?"

I licked my lips and thought over all of my teen years, picking apart anything that Monroe could use against me and, more importantly, Corbin. "I started masturbating at twelve. I kissed another guy after the first. I let a guy touch me once, but his dad came home and we had to stop. I—"

"That's enough," Monroe cut into my ramblings with a raise of his hand. "I don't need to know all of that."

I pursed my lips and slowly nodded, unsure if I'd said too much and let Monroe in on the secret that I felt like an idiot right then. Or maybe Monroe had already figured that out for himself. He did seem pretty perceptive.

Monroe took a deep breath and sighed. A moment later the hard boss was gone and in his place, I saw a man who looked nearly concerned for me, if I could actually believe Monroe could care about a stranger so easily. He didn't seem like the kind of person that would. Not that he was cold, exactly, but he seemed more practical than that.

"Do you really want to go through with this?" he asked.

I nodded, but that wasn't full truth. So I shrugged. "I don't have a choice if I want to be a pilot. This is my one shot."

"That's not really what I asked," Monroe said after a long moment, during which neither of us spoke. I heard a door close and flushed, realizing whoever Dion was, he'd heard everything I'd said. I sank into the chair and tried not to let that bother me. "Do you like the idea of selling your body to a complete stranger in exchange for a large stack of credits?"

I looked away from Monroe's searching gaze and shook my head. "No. Not really. But to get the chance to be a pilot, I'll do it."

Monroe nodded and rose from his chair. I looked up and followed his careful movements with curiosity. When Monroe said nothing more, I became worried. "Is that it? Am I done now? Did I do something wrong?" I asked.

Monroe went to a small side table and returned with a black metal box. "No, we're not done yet. Not quite anyway. I need to take your blood for the test, and then you'll be given a vaccine."

"For what?" I asked even as I rolled my sleeve up and offered my arm to Monroe.

He bent over me and gently pressed a small circle to my skin. "To protect you from diseases." I didn't feel anything at first, and then it pinched, and I instinctively pulled away, but Monroe's hand on my wrist stopped me. With my mouth hanging open, I looked up at Monroe as the pinch turned into a bone-deep pain that brought tears to my eyes and made my chin tremble. I had not cried in front of anyone since Corbin and I had stood together at our parents' funeral and would not start now, but the urge to let the tears go was there, and I hated that.

"Easy," Monroe gently told me, cupping my cheek. "You're doing fine. Let the test run itself."

"Is that—" I licked my lips but didn't move my head out of Monroe's hold. "Is that what it's doing?" I asked.

Monroe nodded. "It is analyzing every structure in your body for impurities. When it is done, I will have a complete workup on you that will rival even your most thorough doctor's. If it tells me you are fit to work, then you will be given the vaccine."

"How much longer will it take?" I asked, the pain lessening as a slow warmth began to flood through my arm.

Monroe rested his hip against the desk. "Not much longer now." His hand dropped from my cheek, and for a moment, I wished he hadn't moved it away. Monroe kept his hand on my wrist, and though I wasn't trying to think about it, I brought my fingers back to trace Monroe's hand.

"Flirting with me won't get you any more special attention than you already get, and virgin or no, I'll still make you scrub the toilets if you piss me off," Monroe said with a wicked smile.

I quickly put my hand flat on the desk. I hadn't really meant to flirt with him. It was far more likely I'd simply wanted to touch him. Pale skin was rare, especially in this sector, where those like me were far more common.

"Sorry," I mumbled, instantly feeling embarrassed.

Monroe smirked at me. "It's fine. Everyone tries it at first. And I was half tempted to see if you'd allow a kiss. I have yet to kiss a Sythe."

That surprised me, and I frowned up at him. "But haven't you and Corbin…?" I shrugged, letting my words trail off and not really wanting to talk about my brother having sex with a man I could barely stop looking at.

Chuckling, Monroe shook his head. "Corbin drew the line early on, and I've never crossed it. He works here, enjoys his time with his clients, but isn't one to easily take someone to his bed outside of work."

I settled down and let that knowledge comfort me.

"Tell me, though, why aren't you as reactive as your brother? It is a common quality among Sythe and one of the reasons he is so popular here. People who have yet to experience a Sythe for themselves may think you're like everyone else, but I've seen the people after your brother is done with them. They're fulfilled and pleased beyond measure. If something happened to you to make that part of yourself diminished, something I need to know about, I'd appreciate being told so I can let bidders be aware of it."

28

Monroe sounded curious, though not judgmental, and I appreciated that. "I am. I just hide it better and can control it," I revealed. Monroe didn't look convinced and so I opened myself up slightly for him. And in that instant, I remembered why I'd made the choice to block as much of my sense of touch as possible as heat prickled along the place on my wrist where we were connected. I pursed my lips and crossed my legs, trying to avoid the physical evidence of the desire Monroe's touch ignited on my skin. I'd felt this before, of course. Each person came with their own bit of heat that I instantly reacted to, but I'd never felt it quite this strongly before. My eyes closed and my head fell to the side as I trembled. It was embarrassing to be so reactive, especially after such a simple touch. But Monroe had asked, and he was right. I knew how much Sythes were wanted in relationships because of our ability to feel things that much brighter. Maybe this would make him start the bidding higher. Maybe—

He removed his hand, and I looked up at him as my body slowly came back to normal.

"How much of that was voluntary?" Monroe asked me, sounding critical.

I shrugged. "Possibly a mix but mostly it wasn't. I spend so much time keeping that part of myself in check, it's easy to control either way." I wouldn't admit to Monroe how much touching him made me want him in a way I hadn't felt before. It scared me, and I shifted away from Monroe now that the intoxicating heat had left my mind.

"Fascinating," Monroe said, putting his hand back on my arm. Before the heat could flare to life within me again, though, I quickly shut it down as much as I could. But it wasn't the heat that made me move toward Monroe or want to put my hand on him.

Monroe looked away from the testing spot he was examining and licked his lips as my gaze met his. "You look interested."

"In what?" I asked him, not looking away.

Monroe smirked. "Me."

I swallowed thickly and managed to nod before Monroe leaned toward me. "Open yourself up for me again," he whispered. A heartbeat later I had, and Monroe's mouth was on mine. As stars exploded in my mind, Monroe cupped my cheek, and I gasped as fire raced down my neck. I parted my lips, letting Monroe into my mouth as his tongue sought entrance. I tilted my head back, eagerly taking more as Monroe deepened our kiss.

There was a pinch on my arm that I quickly ignored in favor of focusing on kissing Monroe, but a second later, pain sliced through my skin where the test had been, and I tore my mouth away, gasping and reaching across my chest to blindly grab at my throbbing arm. Monroe bent his head to place a kiss on my forehead before stepping away.

"You distracted me," I gasped, realization coming quickly.

Monroe didn't deny it as he retook his chair and placed the small patch on a reader. "You expected something else?"

I pursed my lips and looked away, knowing what I had wanted and what I had thought was happening but not wanting to tell him that. I felt tricked and vulnerable, which was never good, especially when I was already on edge.

"Come on, don't be so sour. It isn't an attractive look for you. Besides, this was never going further than a kiss. I couldn't very well damage your virginity."

I glared at him but stayed silent. Minutes later the machine reading the test beeped, and Monroe nodded as he read the results. "You're healthy, though you probably already knew that. Now give me your other arm."

My glare still steady on Monroe, I did as I was told and made sure my nerves were as shut down as I could possibly make them as Monroe put a shiny silver tool against my skin.

"This'll pinch, but it won't be nearly as bad as the test," Monroe said gently.

I wanted to thank him for going easy on me and warning me this time like he hadn't before. But I wasn't about to give the man I was currently really angry at that much satisfaction. Like he'd promised, though, the vaccine was a slight prick, but it hardly felt like anything compared to the test.

"What now?" I asked as I pulled back.

Monroe put the tools away in the black box and set it off to the side of his desk. "Now we talk about what you want from the person who will be your first." The holocard was brought back to the center of the desk, and he bent over to read something I couldn't see from my angle. "What do you desire?"

"Credits," I replied bluntly, not knowing what else Monroe was getting it.

He chuckled and shook his head. "This is your time to get as specific as you want to. The more you do, the smaller you make your pool, but Asiq only entertains a certain level of clientele, so there are very few things you have to be afraid of. So think about it. Man or woman?"

I cringed. "Man. I'm not like my brother, though I didn't know he was bi. Maybe he just is for work."

"He's not. He doesn't have sex with the women he spends time with."

Surprised, I frowned at Monroe. "Then…."

Monroe sat back in his chair. "Can you keep your client's information private?" I nodded. "The woman your brother is currently engaged with recently lost her son. Corbin is the same age as her son was. They talk, sometimes they dance. She shows him baby pictures, and often she cries while he holds her. She's been coming regularly while he's at work and gets a special rate because he agrees to take less from her since he likes to spend time with her as well. In a way I think she reminds him of what it was like to have a mother, though from talking to him, she and your mother were nothing alike."

I had no idea my brother could be like that for anyone, but still I was suspicious. "How do you know that?"

31

Monroe smiled at him. "All of my employees talk to me. Additionally, I have cameras set up in each room. They are activated when a client is admitted and turn off when they leave. It is as much for the protection of the men in my employ as the clients they entertain."

Blushing deeply, I had no idea what to say to that.

But Monroe wasn't done. "A recording can be made of your first time if you wish."

The color in my cheeks darkened, and I shrank into my chair as far as I could go. "Uh...."

"Don't decide that now. Back to your clients. Any races you do not wish to service?" Monroe continued, cutting off what would have likely been unintelligible mumblings from me.

"None that I know of."

Monroe nodded. "Are you into pain? Blood?"

"I don't think so. I mean, I've never done it, so...." I shrugged, unsure of myself, and barely managed to hold back a shudder at the idea of having someone like that be with me for his first time.

"I'll put the cutoff at spanking for your protection. Most of our clients don't come here for that anyway, as there is a darker club for that here on Wish, but a virgin is a special treat and will attract many kinds of clients, so it is best to put something in there just in case."

I smiled and was glad Monroe was thinking of my well-being when I had no idea how to do it for myself in this situation. "I would like my face not to be included in the ads." Monroe looked up, seeming surprised, and I felt silly for even requesting it. Maybe this would be the thing that made Monroe throw me out. Hopefully the guy in the kitchen was nice to me while I worked there over the next two weeks, since I couldn't get home without Corbin taking me back in the shuttle. I didn't have any money to get a ride from the shuttle service that went between the station and Wish. When I thought about being in the kitchen, though, I nearly sighed. I could barely make noodles, so I wasn't completely sure how well that would go if Monroe did decide to put me there.

"Explain," Monroe said, crossing his arms over his muscular chest.

I bit my bottom lip as I tried to come up with some kind of an explanation that would work for him without making me look and sound like a complete idiot. "Well, see, I'm going to be in classes, and I don't want people recognizing me as the guy that sold himself to get in. If that makes sense. I don't mind the guy who pays me knowing since that's kind of unavoidable, but everyone else I'd kind of like to avoid. Maybe?"

Monroe's expression softened, and he nodded. "Of course. It might even add a bit of mystery to the auction. All ads will show you from your cheek down to your waist. Deal?"

I quickly nodded and was glad Monroe had agreed with me.

"Stand up. We'll start with the pictures now." Monroe got to his feet, and I quickly did as well. I stood in the middle of the room with my hands in my pockets, waiting for Monroe to tell me what to do next. "Take off your shirt," Monroe instructed me. "And unbutton your pants."

My mouth fell open as I stared at Monroe. "No," I quickly protested, curling my hands into fists at my sides.

Monroe rolled his eyes. "Have you ever bothered to look at our ads? What do you think they have on them? I don't run an establishment full of saints here."

I pursed my lips. No, I hadn't looked because I didn't want to accidentally stumble across one of Corbin's ads. But I could imagine what they looked like, and in that moment I could have guessed how stupid and naive Monroe probably thought I was being.

Feeling ridiculous for thinking I'd be able to undress for the man who was going to have sex with me in two weeks without freaking out, I yanked off my shirt and pulled open my pants in a not so subtle act of false bravery and defiance. I wasn't being exposed below my waist, and logically I knew that. And yet I still felt completely naked to the point where I had to cross my arms over my chest to keep from putting my hands over the zipper for my pants.

"You Sythe have such lovely purple skin," Monroe said, stepping toward me. There was a small camera across from us, noisily snapping pictures, and I tried not to let the loud clicking bother me as Monroe moved to my side.

"You want to be in the ad too?" I asked, feeling defensive as Monroe ran his fingertips down my exposed arm.

Monroe twitched his nose at me. "Only when necessary. You're supposed to look like a virgin, and while you've got the whole unsure about yourself thing down perfectly, this angry act isn't going to help you get the money you need. Not in the least."

"It's not an act," I replied uncomfortably.

Monroe's brows lifted, and he smoothed his hand down my chest to my stomach. "Let yourself feel, Thierry. Tempt the men into wanting you. Make them think about you on your knees in front of them, their hands in your hair, their cock buried in your mouth." Flushing brightly, I pursed my lips and ducked my head. I didn't know how to look like that.

"How?" I asked.

Monroe smiled at me, and I tried to relax. "You're attracted to me, aren't you?"

Nodding, I wasn't sure where this was going but figured lying would be a bad move right then. "Sure."

"Then open yourself up, feel again, and imagine what it would be like with me," Monroe offered, at which I nearly lost my breath. "Do whatever you need to do to get the shot. You're not in this for the pleasure, so focus on your career. I'm sure you can muster up one sexy look I can use for your ad if it means getting you the career of your dreams. Am I right?"

I forced myself to nod and slowly let myself feel again. I pictured Monroe and me together and sighed softly as he traced his fingers over the waist of my pants. Far too quickly, though, Monroe pulled his hand back, and I was left alone with my brightly flaming nerves once again, reaching out for contact before I had a chance to quiet them. My nerves were a part of me, but nearly as another sense beyond the five most people seemed to have. Having something more wasn't abnormal for the people I knew, but this extreme reaction to touch, where I was nearly blinded by pleasure and desperate to have more, seemed to be exclusive to us Sythes.

I looked across the room to see Monroe smiling down at a holographic image. "Perfect. You can get dressed now."

"What now?" I asked as I straightened my shirt over my pants.

Monroe turned off the camera and put the picture on his desk. "If you were one of my men, you would now be entering into training with a more experienced employee, who would teach you how to talk with clients, dance to seduce them, and generally act in a way that is pleasing to the people who come to visit us. But since you are not, now I get to work on building an ad for you, setting up your auction, and inviting some of my best clients to bid. You'll have your money in two weeks and be on your way. I can promise you that. So from now until I call for you, you need to eat, relax, and not have sex with the other men here. Think you can do that?"

"Yeah. Of course," I quickly said, backing toward the door.

Monroe nodded. "Good. Let yourself out and find your room. It's thirteen. Your brother is in twelve. The door will respond to your fingerprints, now that they've been received with your file from school."

I'd forgotten those had been taken. "Bye. And thanks, Monroe."

"Don't thank me. You're about to make us both a lot of money."

I wasn't sure how he had the confidence to say that, but I found myself trusting him anyway. I didn't really have much of a choice if I wanted the chance to become a pilot. "Why would someone pay so much for me?" I asked him out of curiosity.

"You don't think you're worth it?"

Honestly, I didn't. But I wasn't about to tell him that. "I'm just one person. A virgin, sure. But—"

"You're Sythe. That's enough. Because of how you are with people when your kind have sex, I know the kind of prices you'll bring. Clearly you don't think being Sythe is that special, but from someone that doesn't get to see someone experience pleasure as easily as your kind seem to, I can tell you that any price you get will be more than worth it. Most people show pleasure. They moan, they gasp, they sigh. That is normal. One touch with you, though, seems to be the equivalent of the kind of pleasure most people have when they orgasm. For someone that enjoys seeing their partner experience everything they do to them in such a heightened degree, this will be the experience of a lifetime. Now, I assume you can find your way. The doors have numbers on them. Go find yours."

Monroe sat down at the desk and began working. The tight ball in my gut had eased considerably, but it still hadn't gone away completely, and I wasn't sure it would until my time at Asiq was up and I was back home in my own bed.

CHAPTER
FOUR

ON A busy Saturday night at Asiq two weeks later, I sat with the others guys, eating a frozen lemon treat as music played around us. There were plenty of customers too, and I tried to keep to the shadows after refusing advances from them. It had gotten easier as the days passed, but I still jumped when someone thought it was okay to randomly put their hands on my knee or to try to kiss me, like that was the only thing they needed to do in order to change my mind. What was nice, though, was that enough of the people were regulars and it seemed I didn't have to tell that many no. Most of them appeared to figure it out after a while.

Either that, or I wasn't that good to look at, and Monroe was wrong about how easy this would be for us. I tried not to let those kinds of thoughts come in too often, but they were still there, and I didn't have much control over them.

The guys next to me got up to dance, and some of the customers clapped as they started rubbing up against each other. I blushed and looked away, very sure I'd never be comfortable dancing like that in front of others. And then I got a bit sick as I realized Corbin probably did that all the time to entertain the people who came to see him. At least my brother wasn't around right then, since he was with a client. I might have had to leave the room then.

I ended up standing anyway when I finished eating the icy treat, and I needed another one. Monroe had said to eat and so I had been doing just that. Two weeks with his food, and I felt full and relaxed. I hung out with the guys, since most of them were pretty cool and just normal people, and I read some too. Honestly it was a bit boring, but maybe if I had actually been working, I would have been able to stay focused. As it was I had far too much downtime, and since I wasn't supposed to leave Asiq, on Monroe's orders and probably in case I decided to run back home, that meant I had too much time in which I had nothing better to do than think.

This always quickly dissolved into me wondering what in the universe I was doing there as I was about to be selling my virginity to a stranger. The first few days after we arrived, I was clear-headed, and it was something I was going to do so I could have the future I wanted. Then it became this thing—this looming, scary thing—I was headed toward with no way to stop it, and like a black hole, I felt it would suck me in and then I'd become nothing.

I tried not to think like that, but the thoughts were there, and they'd been increasing as the days counted down. With less than two hours until midnight on the night before I was to lose my virginity, I could think of little else than the catastrophe I'd gotten myself in. And I still didn't know if anyone had bid on me or not.

That's how I found myself in front of Monroe's office with a lemon treat in one hand and my other raised to knock on the door.

"You can come in, Thierry," he called when I started to turn away.

"How did you know it was me?" I asked after stepping inside the room. I closed the door behind me and came over to sit across from him at his desk as I had the first time. He was bent over his holoscreen, looking at what appeared to be a series of numbers, but I couldn't be sure from the angle.

"I have cameras everywhere," Monroe reminded me. He lifted his head and put the holoscreen to the side. "What do you need?"

I chewed on my bottom lip until he started tapping his fingers on the desk, a clear sign from him I was wasting his time.

"Did anyone bid on me at all?" I asked shyly, instantly worried about his answer.

Monroe smiled and handed me the holoscreen. "You're in luck. The time to bid is counting down now. That number in green, there at the bottom, is the current bid."

I stared at it for a long time before glancing back at him. And then I went right back to looking at the screen a second later. "But that's…. Someone is willing pay twenty thousand more than I need just to have sex with me?"

"For a virgin, yes. As I told you in our first meeting, virgins are a rare treat in this industry, and in the outside world as well, I'm assuming. Some people never get to enjoy them. Others seek them out. You've got something people are willing to pay quite a bit for, and all you have to do is take off your clothes and have sex with a stranger."

I gulped and folded my hands in my lap. "That's the part I'm struggling with the most," I told him honestly.

The holoscreen beeped, and he looked down at it, nodded, then looked up at me. "Is it that you'll have to be vulnerable with them, that you think it will hurt, or that you don't want to run into them on the street in a year?"

I flushed brightly at having him lay my fears out like that so simply, like he was asking me what I wanted to eat instead of what was actually happening. "The first two for sure, and I hadn't even considered the last one yet, but now I am." I sighed miserably and leaned forward to drop my forehead onto the desk. "It'll be okay, won't it?" I asked without looking up.

Monroe chuckled, and I closed my eyes. I couldn't believe he was laughing at me at a time like this, when I was really struggling with my decision.

"You want reassurances, to know they'll take care of you, and they'll still respect you and want you when they're through with you?" he asked. I heard the mocking in his voice, and I shuddered, knowing I wouldn't get any of that my first time.

"I'm not stupid," I said as I lifted my head.

Monroe nodded. "I don't doubt you think you're smart. But you need to start acting like it. This is a business transaction. You have inherent value, you want money, you sell what you have, which is your virginity, and you get paid for it. And very well too, I might add. You will be safe here, but how you feel about it afterward and how you deal with any feelings that pop up in the future are things you need to get a handle on outside these walls."

"Just a business transaction...." I repeated.

"Very much so. Now, if you'd like to stay a few minutes longer, you'll get to see the end of the auction instead of wondering about it overnight."

I leaned forward as he turned the holoscreen around so I could see it too. The seconds were counting down, and I braced myself against the edge of the table to keep from falling over. At first the number jumped as more people placed bids, but then it slowed, and when the countdown ended and a winning bid was announced, the winner had been the bidder for most of the time I'd been watching the holoscreen.

Monroe spun the holoscreen around to face him. "Excellent. That is a very good price, and you'll still have enough to go to school after I take my cut. This bidder was so set on winning he actually placed automatic bids and sent me a note shortly after the auction began."

I wasn't good at suppressing my emotions, but I didn't even try to hide my surprise at hearing that. "Automatic bids? And what did his note say?"

Monroe tapped at the screen and pulled up something. I was hoping he'd let me read it, but he didn't turn it around to let me. "He says he is a powerful man and wishes to remain anonymous. I am to have a meal prepared to his liking, and he will arrive with a hood over his face to cover his features. He will not speak to you, and you will not know his name. You two will have a private dinner, and I will have you bathed and dressed as he has wished. And, to answer your question, an automatic bid is when someone places a bid that is as high as they will go, and that number is kept secret. Everyone else bids, and his bid is automatically increased by a certain amount each time as long as it remains the highest bid. It lets people who are willing to pay be assured they will most likely win."

"Oh." I needed a minute to let all of that sink in.

"Your brother is done for the day. If you need to speak to someone, I suggest you join him."

"Are you kicking me out of your office?" I asked, trying to sound like I was joking but not really managing. The reality I was in had started to sink in, and once again, I wasn't sure I could actually handle this part.

Monroe nodded toward the door. "Yes."

I went from feeling like I was drowning to being annoyed. "Jerk," I muttered as I got to my feet.

"Yes, I am. But I am the jerk who just made you rich, so try to be a little respectful," he chided me.

I blushed deeply and shook my head. "Sorry. You weren't supposed to hear that."

Monroe looked up at me and gave me a quick nod. "Be that as it may, I intentionally pushed you. When you're angry you snap out of whatever bad emotions are bothering you. I need you level-headed so I can't keep you angry until tomorrow, but a depressed, frightened virgin won't be a good experience for the bidder either. So figure it out for yourself, and make it work. I will not have an angry customer on my hands because you had second thoughts. This will happen. He has already paid. When you're done, I'll pay you. That way you have incentive not to run away tonight."

I gave him a cold glare. "I wouldn't do that."

"Either way, the door is there, and I have work to do. Good-bye."

Rolling my eyes, I left his office to find my brother. I tried his room first but found him waiting in mine when he opened the door and handed me a hunk of chocolate. "Here, try this," he told me.

"How'd you get in my room?" I asked.

He sat down on my bed, which was bigger than any I'd ever had before, and shrugged. "I tried my thumbprint on the door, and it worked for me too. I guess Monroe never changed it over from when I had access to both of them. How's the bidding going now?"

I lay down on the bed beside him and pulled one of the pillows under my arm as I nibbled on the chocolate. It wasn't something I'd had before coming to Wish, but in Asiq there were little wrapped bars in nearly every room. I'd had a lot of them, knowing I wouldn't get to indulge in the treat after I left.

"It's over. Some guy who doesn't want me to know his identity won." I finished off my chocolate. "Is that weird?"

Corbin shook his head and lay down next to me. For once, when we were relaxing like this together, I didn't feel as if he was going to push me out of bed by moving. It was one of the many little pleasures I'd found here in Asiq, and a big part of me was afraid that tomorrow that would all come crashing down and I would hate that I'd ever come to Wish or had such a stupid idea as to sell my virginity.

"It's really not. I mean, I have guys all the time who want to keep who they are a secret. Normally that means blindfolding me, but I got this guy once in a skintight suit that went all over his body. I didn't know who he was. I could see him every day and would have no idea. That's kind of nice, though, in its own way."

"It is?"

"Yeah. Because if you knew who he was, and he was someone famous or something, and you didn't like it after you'd done it, then every time you heard his name or saw an image of him, it might bug you. This way you won't have any of that. You can just have sex with him and be done. Simple."

"Huh." I hadn't thought about it like that. "That's true."

"I know."

I had a lot of questions, none of them I wanted to voice aloud and most of them having to deal with my brother's work here, which I didn't want to know about at all. Except I did kind of need to know about it, at least a little. And so I picked my questions as carefully as possible.

"Have you ever regretted coming here?" I asked.

He put his hands behind his head and stared up at the ceiling. "Honestly? No. It's not a traditional way of making a living, but when I first talked to Monroe after seeing an ad one day, we were in a bad place. I was doing that mining job where I was feeling sick a lot, remember that one?" I nodded. I'd been young, but I remembered him coming home and feeling like crap but still going to work the next day because if he missed a day, he would have been automatically fired.

"So you like it, then?"

"Yeah. That weird for you?"

I nodded. I couldn't imagine someone liking having sex with even one stranger, much less dozens, or hundreds, or…. I shuddered, not wanting to think about how many people my brother had been with. That was definitely not something I ever wanted to know.

"You might like it. You never know. I mean, it is pretty freeing to know that when someone comes to me, all they want is that moment. There's no cheating, no drama, no arguments. It's about giving and receiving pleasure, and so even though I don't have relationships with the people I'm with, it feels like I do sometimes. Like I get the best parts of being with someone without any of the bad ones."

"But you don't get the other stuff, do you?" I asked.

"Like what? Dates and things?"

I nodded. He smiled at me. "I still get dates. Asiq is less by the hour and more by the experience, if that makes sense. So if a guy just wants to have sex with me, fine. That can be done, and he gets booked for that. But there are people who come for dinner or dancing, or to sit and talk awhile. Generally they get sex too, but that's not all they come here for, and so they pay more. Or there are some who just want to talk."

"Like Mrs. Marsden? Monroe mentioned her the first day I was here," I explained when he gave me a surprised look.

"Didn't know he'd share secrets like that. But yes, like her, where all she wants is someone to listen to her talk about her son. Her husband is gone too, she had no other family but him, and most of her friends aren't around either, so she comes, she visits, and she talks to me."

That kind of time sounded nice to me. But whoever had bid on me hadn't spent that much money just to talk to someone. "Will you be ready to leave tomorrow as soon as I am?"

"We fly out at nine tomorrow night. If you're not ready, though, I can wait."

"And then what happens?" I asked him.

He shrugged. "Then we go home, you pay your tuition, and I sit on my butt for two weeks."

I smiled, knowing that's exactly what we'd do as soon as we got home. But that's not what I'd been asking about. "No, what happens here?"

"Oh. Well, we change our sheets and blankets and things between clients anyway, but when our two weeks are over, Monroe brings in a cleaning crew to get everything really nice. Asiq is closed down for four hours in the middle of the night for cleaning, then it's business as usual. Most of the guys don't realize that and think Monroe needs a few hours without any of us here, but I stayed late one time with a client for a long dinner date with dancing and saw the cleaners come in."

It made sense things would get done like that, even from my extremely limited perspective. "Do you think tomorrow will go okay?"

Corbin shrugged, and I wished he could give me an absolute answer, like he had when we were children and I was worried. "I think you'll get what you need out of it, and if you need to talk when you're done, we can. I don't think it'll be the best time of your life, or that you'll be wanting to come back here and do this full-time,

44

but if you look at it like he's a stepping stone to what you really want in life, you may be able to suck it up."

I considered his words. I could do this. I was sure of it. And Corbin was right. This guy was something that had to happen for me to get to where I was supposed to be as a pilot. I wouldn't be suffering through it, but I also wouldn't be having a great time either. I'd be somewhere in the middle, and as long as I could still look at myself in the mirror after it was over, things would be okay. That was my plan, and I thought it was a good one. I was actually feeling decent and almost optimistic about what the next day would bring. That was, until I went to bed some hours later and found myself lying awake as I stared up at the ceiling, a litany of worries racing through my mind.

I couldn't do it, but I had to. I could run, but then Monroe would have caught me and fired Corbin.... I turned on my side and sighed loudly as I realized that as much as I didn't want to go through with it, I needed the money. A little voice at the back of my mind said maybe it wouldn't be as awful as I was imagining it to be. Maybe it could be something good. Maybe my first time didn't have to be horrible.

Or, I figured, more likely I'd end up hating every second of it and wishing I'd never thought of this stupid plan.

CHAPTER FIVE

AT JUST after four the next day, Monroe came to my room, where I'd been reading the latest sector news on my holoscreen.

"Come on, it's time to get ready," he told me.

And just like that, I was up and heading out of the room. "Where are we going?" I asked as we headed down a series of corridors I hadn't been in before. Asiq was large, being over three stories tall with at least a dozen rooms on each level, but I hadn't realized the door we'd gone through to get to this hallway wasn't actually a way into a room.

"I have a series of guest rooms back here for when important people come to visit and wish to keep their identities a secret," he told me without looking at me. "Given the nature of your client's other requests, I felt this would be best. There is a door at the back of the building, which he will enter through. You two will have complete privacy, just as I'm sure you'd want as well."

I realized that I did. This was scary enough without wondering if everyone in the brothel could hear us as well. "You can still see us, though, right? With your cameras, I mean?"

He stopped at a brightly painted red door and frowned. "Would you rather I couldn't?"

I leaned against the wall and shook my head. "With you watching…." I took a breath and glanced at the door before giving my attention back to him. "I'm scared. But maybe with you watching, he might not try anything."

Monroe slowly nodded. "He wouldn't anyway, even if I weren't monitoring every room in this place. When I opened the auction, I only invited loyal customers to bid, and every one of them is a complete gentleman. Other places on Wish may allow just anyone off the street to come in, but I do not."

He opened the door, and I tried not to see the big four-poster bed that took up most of the room. Instead I focused on the little things, like a table and two chairs that stood against the wall, or a cobalt blue treat dish I plucked a wrapped piece of chocolate out of.

"How do you keep bad people from coming in?" I asked.

"The main doors, unlike the ones Corbin brought you through on your first day here, have built-in automatic scanners that check that person's features against the universal database for past criminal activity, along with known familiars who may also have a questionable history. If a flag goes up, the doors don't open and an electronic voice lets them know they aren't allowed in because of their public record. People can appeal this decision, but most know it'll be a waste of their time and mine. Now, if there aren't any more questions pertaining to your personal security, let's get on with tonight. Shall we?"

I bit my lip, wishing I could still run away and pretend this wasn't about to happen. "Your client has requested that you bathe and get yourself ready using the items in the bathroom. He picked them out especially for this night. I must say, he does have expensive taste. It is good you were able to catch the attention of someone like him. Most people have sex for the first time with people they like but don't love and who don't love them back. There's little difference to that than what you'll be doing tonight, only you get your future out of it, whereas they may never hear from their partners again. It is a smart decision you've made, Thierry. I know you wish to hide what you're doing here from the rest of the world, but there is no shame in making the best decision for yourself, given the options available to you."

I appreciated what he was saying, but that didn't mean I was going to go around announcing what I'd done to get into the academy. "After I get cleaned up, what do I put on?" I asked, moving through the evening in my mind. I didn't have to ask where the bathroom was since there was an open door to my left that showed me glimpses of it.

Monroe moved to the bathroom and pushed the door farther open, enough for me to see a stack of towels on a low bench next to the tub and a robe hanging underneath a high window. "Shower. The toiletries are there already. Just press the buttons on the dispensers for what you need. Then brush your teeth, wear the robe." He brought me back out of the bathroom.

"A meal is being prepared right now, again at his request. This is his fantasy, and I have everyone involved working to his specifications. While you're getting prepared, the food will be brought in and laid out for you both. You will wait to eat until he has arrived."

"It won't get cold by then?" I asked Monroe, who quickly shook his head.

"Your client hasn't requested anything that would need to be kept warm. The necessities you'll need are in a basket next to the bed."

I wasn't sure what he meant, so I went over and saw dozens of little bottles of lube. "I think you went overboard."

"I keep a variety of brands, tastes, and smells on hand in case clients want to experiment. Now, Thierry, do you have any questions about tonight?"

I crossed my arms, then fidgeted until I shoved my hands into my pockets. I was trying not to look as nervous as I felt, but I was pretty sure I was failing miserably. "When do I get paid?" I blurted, and then cringed at the crassness of my words.

Monroe chuckled and went to the door. "The balance is already in your account, minus my cut, of course."

I nodded, remembering how much he'd gotten paid. "What do I do after he's gone?"

"Stay here. I will come to fetch you again, and you'll be on your way. Don't rush this, though. This may not be your idea of a grand time, but it is for him, and also, this is your first time. You only get one of those. Make it something to remember. Make it the best it can possibly be, because even if you lie to some future partner and tell them they are your first, this will always be the truth, and you don't want to regret this moment."

I knew what he was saying, and he was making sense, but I still couldn't completely give in to the idea that I might enjoy any of what was about to happen. I'd endure it, and I'd fake it so the guy didn't get angry at me, but that was more self-preservation than anything else. In the end all I wanted was my money, and I was just a few short hours away from leaving this place behind for good.

"Thanks for setting this up," I told Monroe, knowing it was a necessary thing to say. I'd needed him to get what I wanted in life. None of this would have happened without his help, and I hoped he knew I appreciated it, despite how nervous and scared I was.

"You'll do fine. I'll be back in a couple hours. Hurry up and get ready. You only have an hour before I expect him to arrive."

I didn't have a way to find out what time it was, but I made sure to go as quickly as I could through my usual routine after Monroe left. The client had picked out something fruity smelling for me to wash with, and the same lingering scent was in the shampoo I used. I shaved my face, not that there was much hair there to worry about, and left the little trail on my lower stomach alone, not having been told to remove it.

I brushed my teeth, and then, since I'd be sharing this bathroom, hung up the towel wrapped around my waist and donned a robe that was too big for me. I returned to the room to find the food already laid out for us, just as Monroe had promised. I eyed the

49

selection of meats, cheeses, and fruits greedily. There was even a bottle of wine waiting, though I usually didn't drink.

I briefly considered having a drink to calm down before he arrived, but then discarded the idea. I was afraid of how the liquor would play with my nerves. I needed to be in control, but I knew I wouldn't be shutting myself down around him either. He'd paid to have sex with a Sythe, and I'd give him that. He was paying for my education; maybe it would be a fair trade in his eyes. He'd certainly spent enough on the evening.

I wondered what my client did for a living. Average people couldn't afford the food he'd picked out, and definitely not the wine either. Maybe I'd be meeting some rich diplomat who was on Wish briefly before going off to negotiate a peace treaty between cultures I'd never even heard of.

I was still musing over this when there was a knock on the door. It might have been Monroe, but I knew it likely wasn't. When I opened the door to a man dressed in a fancy black suit, my suspicions were confirmed.

"Hi," I squeaked. The nervousness wasn't an act at all.

He wore a mask wrapped the whole way around his head, and since there were mesh coverings over his eyes, I couldn't see what color they were. The only exposed part of his face was his mouth and really, mouths were generic enough that if I ever saw this man again without his mask on, I wouldn't recognize him.

"Won't you come in?" I said, remembering my manners.

He pulled the corners of his mouth up into a little smile, then walked past me into the room. He was fully dressed, and I was in a short robe that barely came down to my thighs, leaving me feeling as naked as if I hadn't had anything on at all. Since he'd picked out everything else, I assumed he'd chosen the robe too, so maybe that was his intention all along. If he wanted me uneasy and unnerved, he was getting his wish.

He sat down at the little table, and I joined him. I waited for him to pour us each a glass of wine and put some of the cheese and meat on his plate before I got some for myself as well. And then we ate in silence that was so uncomfortable, I found myself wanting to babble just to fill it. So I did.

"Hi. So, I'm Thierry."

He stopped eating for a moment to raise his head and look at me before going back to a bit of meat.

"Thank you for bidding on me...." That wasn't weird at all to say. Oh yes, it was.

He gave me a little nod, then ate part of an apple.

The silence stretched between us for a while longer as we ate. Well, he ate. I picked at my food because I was too nervous to do much else with it. I tried the wine, and it was good, but I couldn't have more than a few sips before I knew I was done with it.

"I'm going to become a pilot," I said. It was harder than I'd thought to have a conversation with myself. "That's what I'll be using the money for. I thought you might want to know that." I didn't have much else to say to someone I didn't know and who wasn't speaking to me.

I nibbled on a berry, then licked my fingers clean. He'd stopped eating, and I waited to see what he was going to do. He reached over and pulled my finger out of my mouth, which was weird, but what was even stranger was that he then put my finger in his mouth and sucked on it a little before releasing my hand. I shivered and put my hands in my lap. I hadn't opened myself up to him at all yet, but I knew I would, because that was only fair. If I hadn't been closed off right then, I was sure I would have felt something. I wasn't quite sure what, to be honest, but there was something there.

I'd never been seduced before, if that was even the word for what was happening. He got out of his chair, and I was quick to follow him. He took my hand in his and curled his fingers around mine. I didn't have much experience in this department, and I wished I'd had some so this wouldn't have felt so new and unfamiliar. I stepped toward him to kiss him, since I figured that was what was supposed to happen next, but he turned his head at the last second so my lips landed on his cheek instead. The mask was soft enough, but I didn't like that he was wearing it since it would have been nice to see his face.

I opened myself up and wasn't surprised to find myself instantly reacting to his hand in mine. I was already at a low fire because of how nervous I was, and it didn't help that half of me wanted to run out the door screaming. He reached for the knotted tie on my robe, and stupid me, I backed up, not wanting him to see me naked yet. He didn't yank me back, didn't squeeze my hand, none of that. I was staring at his shoes, shiny black and clean, as I moved toward him and this time when he reached for me, I let him undo my sash. My robe hung open, and I stood there, wondering what he thought of me even though I was still partially covered.

When he let go of my hand, I wanted to cover myself up, but I forced myself to stay still as he went behind me and gently took the robe off my shoulders. I froze when he had me naked, nearly shaking as he walked around me. I felt him watching me, studying me, and I only hoped I measured up to his standards. He kissed me, and I was still so unsure of myself, I didn't touch him at all as he pressed his mouth against mine. He put his hands on my butt and cupped it, pulling me close until I could feel him pressing against my stomach. I opened myself up all the way and felt fire along my veins as warmth moved through me. It was more than him touching me that made me hard, though. It was partially the nervousness too, but when he was kissing me and I allowed myself to feel, I wasn't so afraid. He put one hand under my outer thigh and lifted my leg, bringing it around his hip. He did the same to the other, and I was being lifted and carried over to the bed with his mouth still on mine.

His clothes were soft as they rubbed against my skin, but it wasn't until he'd laid me on the bed and covered me with his body that I really felt him against me. I bit my lip as he lifted his head to suck on my neck. He took his hands away to begin undressing himself, and though I'd had my head turned away as he licked and sucked my neck, I watched him out of the corner of my eye.

He was beautiful because he was a Denobelas, but more than that, he was muscular with tanned skin that was smooth under my fingertips when I got up the nerve to touch his chest. I'd expected him to have some light hairs at least, but he was completely shaven.

He kicked off his shoes, then his pants, and suddenly I was naked with a man I didn't know who was only wearing a hood, and I was trying not to freak out. He must have figured out that something was wrong halfway through my panic session in which I was struggling to breathe because he stopped rubbing himself against me and simply pressed his forehead against mine. He held still for a good five minutes just like that, letting me breathe with neither of us moving, until I thought I was ready again.

"Sorry," I mumbled. "I got a little overwhelmed. It's just...." I licked my lips and tried to come up with something that didn't sound completely stupid. But nothing that came into my mind made it to my lips. So I ended up sounding stupid as I stated the obvious. "It's my first time." He already knew that, but I saw him smile anyway and figured maybe a little panic session wasn't an awful thing, like I'd originally thought.

He started kissing down my body, and I tried to remind myself to breathe through my nerves, through how scared and worried I was, and past the heat that threatened to suffocate me faster than my fear ever could. I worried about being good, being attractive, being big enough. I worried about the sounds I was going to make, if my face would look awful while we were having sex, if I was supposed to have shaved everywhere, like he had.

I was so worried in fact, I nearly missed the moment his mouth closed around the head of my cock. It wasn't a light touch. He put his mouth over me and sucked hard enough I arched off the bed and cried out. I wasn't sure whether glaring at him would be better than kissing him in that moment, so I chose to do neither and gripped the blanket under my fingertips as he slid his mouth down my shaft and sucked me on his way back up.

My noises were weird, I was sure of it. They were probably so completely weird, I was surprised he was still going down on me a few minutes later. But then he stopped, and I wondered why, but I found the good sense not to ask him to keep going. I'd enjoyed that, but I had to remember this wasn't for me. Well, it was, in that I was getting money from it, and I'd be a pilot and explore galaxies. But this experience, this wasn't for me. He'd wanted this, had illustrated it down to what shampoo I washed my hair with before he arrived. This was all about him, and I was just a passenger on this ride.

I kept myself open so I could feel everything, even though I knew he probably wouldn't let me finish. I wanted him to enjoy this, because he was giving me such a huge gift.

He stopped sucking me, and when he came back up, I had my arms open for him. I kissed him, and when he lay down between my legs, I wrapped them around the back of his thighs. He rubbed against me, grinding us together until we'd developed a rhythm, and I was panting in his ear.

Of course, then he chose to move off me and end our kiss. I wondered what he was doing until I saw him go for the basket of lubes. My heart started beating wildly because, logically, I knew what was coming, but that didn't make me any less afraid. I hoped it wouldn't hurt, but I was sure it would. I hoped I wouldn't cry and whimper like a child, and I could pull off being sexy my first time.

Instead of taking me to that point right then, though, he knelt next to my face. I figured out what he wanted when he slid the head of his cock against my lips. I started to get up, but he put his hand on the middle of my chest, stopping me. So I opened my mouth and let him in. It was awkward with him at my side and not letting me get up, but I figured it out well enough. He put his hand in my hair and guided me. I closed my eyes and sucked him. I wasn't good at it, at least I didn't think so, but he didn't make me feel like I was doing anything wrong either.

He let me continue for a few more minutes, then he pulled away. I was sure then we would actually start having sex, but no, I was wrong again. He knelt between my thighs. I was about to ask him what he was doing, realizing he wouldn't have answered me anyway, when he reached under my thighs to pull me forward and he moved backward until I was hanging off the bed, my legs on either side of him. Then he pushed my knees up with strong hands behind them, and before I could figure out exactly what his plan was, he had his mouth on my hole and was licking me.

It was weird, it even tickled a little at first, and before I could relax and just go with it, he was standing up again. He stuck a finger inside of me, and I tensed as I stared up at him. But as he worked the lube into me with first one finger and then another, I tried to relax. This was supposed to happen, I knew, and I had to ease into it. It no longer tickled to have him playing with me there, and I was finding new areas of pleasure I didn't even know I had. I mean, I'd known they were there. I wasn't an idiot. But I'd never played with myself, and I didn't know it would feel like that.

I expected him to turn me over when he went into me, but instead he put one hand underneath my knee and positioned himself with the other. As soon as he went in a little, I whimpered and tensed up. He waited for me. At least I thought that's what he was doing, because he didn't go into me any more until I relaxed again. It hurt, there was no denying that, but it burned more than anything as I stretched around him. When he was in, he put a hand under my other knee and pushed my legs toward the mattress until I gasped. If this was how sex was supposed to be, I really needed to work on my stretching.

He kissed me and slid into me. I put my shaking hands on his shoulders as he lay over me. I'd always known I could say no, even if Monroe had never confirmed that, but as the burning started to ease and a slowly building pleasure replaced that sensation, I knew I wouldn't.

He pushed his tongue into my mouth, and all I could do was get comfortable under him and open up every nerve in my body, giving him everything I had, everything I was. I'd never opened myself up that much before. I usually chose to keep a part of myself reserved and hidden away because this left me vulnerable and exposed. But with him I was already completely exposed, and in a very real and pretty massive way. He knew me better than anyone else in that moment as I lay frightened under him, reacting to his touch even before I knew what to do.

He opened his mouth and bit into my collarbone, and I cried out. I dug my fingers into his shoulders, sure I was scraping them against his skin, but since he didn't stop, neither did I. He lifted himself up enough to wrap a hand around my shaft, and I didn't want to let him go. When he came in me, and I splashed over his hand and my stomach, I nearly cried. My first orgasm with someone else was wonderful, but that wasn't why I was biting my lip to keep from crying after he finished kissing me. It was more that I knew we would be over now. I'd spent so much time worrying about what would happen or being afraid of him hurting me, I hadn't spent enough time enjoying what he had done for me.

When he got up to move away from me, I kept my hand on him. It was hard to let him go. I wanted to try again, show him I would be better, that I wouldn't whine as much when there was pain, that I could handle being stretched by him. But he just leaned down to give me a kiss on my forehead before sliding off the bed. I sat up and watched him go into the bathroom. He was in there for a few minutes, and when he came back, he had a warm, damp towel in his hands that he ran over my stomach and cock.

"Thank you," I mumbled when he'd finished cleaning me. I meant it, not just for the sex, but for everything. I wasn't sure how to tell him that, though. "You didn't have to be nice to me, but you were. I was worried you wouldn't be."

He didn't say anything to that, just nodded and cleaned himself too, before tossing the washcloth on the bed beside me. He got dressed, but he was slow about it, and I got to look my fill of him as he put his pants back on. I should have probably gotten dressed instead of staring at him, but honestly, this was more fun, and as a one-time thing, I wanted to see everything about the guy I'd given my virginity to.

It would have been nice to see his face, but I got a good view of lots of muscle and a smooth body I wish I'd been able to do more to. I wanted to touch him, explore where I wanted to, and put my mouth on him. But I didn't get to, and soon enough he was dressed. He came over and gave me one last kiss, one last pull on my hair, and bent my neck so he could kiss me, a deep kiss that left me panting for more as he pulled his tongue out of my mouth. If his intention had been to make sure I never forgot him, he succeeded with that kiss.

He didn't look back as he left. Didn't wave, didn't do anything. Once the kiss was over, he was out of the door and gone.

It took me a long time to move from that spot, to come back to myself, to remember I had things to do, and they didn't include sitting naked on a bed, wondering why I was upset that a guy who had paid me for sex hadn't said a single word to me. It wasn't a relationship, wasn't anything. It was just sex, and I needed to remember that. I didn't even know his name or what he looked like, but after I showered and put my clothes on, I sort of missed him, as stupid as that sounded. So what if he'd been nice to me? My next boyfriend would be nice to me too. And we'd have sex, and it would be fine. Maybe not like that, but it would be fine. Because that's what normal people did. They didn't pine after a guy who had paid them for their virginity and wish they'd had more time to spend with him. That was insanity, but that was exactly what I was thinking as I sat at the little table and finished off food I couldn't afford and likely wouldn't have again for a good long time, if ever.

CHAPTER SIX

MONROE CAME back for me an hour later, after I had finished the food on the table and was moving over to the bowl of chocolates.

"Hungry?" he teased.

I shrugged and popped another sweet treat into my mouth. "Do you know who he was?" I asked.

He hesitated. "I won't tell you his identity."

I hadn't expected he would. "But you do know it, don't you?"

Monroe gave me a slight nod. "I do. Why?"

"He had a tattoo on his ribs I wanted to ask you about, and I also wanted to make sure you knew who he was before I told you that detail, in case it gave him away." I sat down at the table, and he sat down across from me. It bothered me for a moment that Monroe was in my client's chair, and then I realized how stupid it was of me to think that way.

"Describe the tattoo for me," Monroe said. He leaned forward over the table and crossed his arms.

I frowned, because that was the complicated part. I didn't know how to describe it, because I'd never seen a creature like that before. "It was a bug, I think. No, it was definitely a bug. With a slender body and long wings that were also thin."

Monroe gave a little shrug. "Sounds a little like a dragonfly."

I didn't know what that was. "Huh?"

"Look it up. I'm too busy to give you a biology lesson. I do, however, have time to pass on a request from your client."

I wasn't sure what more he could possibly want from me, but I was willing to listen, so I gave Monroe a nod and waited for him to continue.

"Your client has requested weekly notes from you that will be passed through me and then sent on to him. He is offering you an extra thousand credits per month, to be paid at the end of the month after the fourth letter has arrived and has said that he will continue to pay for these letters as long as you are in school. Is that something you're willing to do?"

I frowned, having no idea why he would want to hear from me. "What would I even say to him?" I mused aloud.

Monroe was starting to look irritated with me. "The weather, how your classes are going, how you annoy people with ridiculous questions, for starters."

I flushed and pursed my lips at him. How Corbin put up with him was beyond me. I wasn't in the mood for him right then, though. I was tired and still reeling from my experience. It was a process, and Monroe wasn't helping.

"I'll agree to that."

Monroe smiled. "Good."

Then something occurred to me. "You're not taking a cut of that, are you?"

He laughed and got up from the table. "No. But I will be the one depositing the money directly into your account, as I did with your share of the money from the auction. It is one more way of keeping his identity a secret."

"Maybe he'll tell me who he is if he ever writes back to me," I said as I got up too. I sort of hoped he would.

Monroe led me back to the main part of Asiq, where I had been staying. "Get your things together. You and Corbin will be off-world in an hour," he said when we'd stopped at the door to my room.

I nodded. "Bye, then."

"Bye." He turned and quickly left me to it.

Corbin and I left right on time, and I sighed as he blasted the heat in the shuttle for me. "How was it?" he asked once we were heading back to our home on the space station.

I shrugged, not entirely sure how to explain what had happened between myself and the man. "It was… nice? Maybe? It wasn't awful anyway. And I got enough for school." That had been the most important part of the whole thing. "Do you ever forget your first?"

Corbin shook his head and glanced at me. "No, not really. You okay?"

I nodded. I was okay. I'd had a good time and that was all that it was. "He wants letters from me."

"Creepy kind of letters?"

I shook my head. "Monroe didn't say what kind of letters the man wanted, just that I was supposed to write to him. He's paying me for them monthly." I took out my holoscreen and sent the money to the academy while I was thinking about it.

Corbin whistled low. "Maybe you should start paying our bills then."

I laughed and settled into my seat. It was a long way home, and without my nervousness to keep me on edge, I slowly drifted off to sleep.

TWO WEEKS later I was finishing up the first week of class. Saying good-bye to Corbin had been hard, but I got a weekend a month off-world, so I'd see him again soon, and he wrote all the time. Being in the academy, going to classes all day, made me feel like selling my virginity had been worth it, like even though it wouldn't be the right choice for everyone, it had made sense for me to do it. Of course I wasn't going to tell any of the people around me that, though.

I turned over on my bed, in a room I shared with three other guys, all about the same age as me, and flipped through my holoscreen. It was late, but it wasn't quite lights out, and everyone else in the dorm was still up. I hadn't become friends with anyone yet, mostly because even there, surrounded by my peers, I was an outsider. They'd all come from this planet, were largely Denobelas, and most of them had been friends for years before getting accepted. I had none of that to back me up, but I hoped maybe when the test scores were posted, and they all saw I could make it there too, and it wasn't some fluke that I'd gotten in, I'd be accepted by some of them. Until that day came, though, I was a loner, which made me pretty miserable, but at least I had Corbin to talk to.

I was on my stomach with the holoscreen in my hands and a pillow propping up my chest as I studied. Even though I didn't fit in, I was loving it at the academy. Everyone was so serious about becoming a pilot and landing the big break that would let them man their own starship that I felt welcome here. I was still the Sythe orphan from somewhere, who didn't have a name, but I was a student too, and that meant something.

And I was learning so much. I wouldn't actually get to pilot anything for at least a year, but I read about ships and galaxies and there was even combat training, which I guessed they thought everyone needed to know sooner or later. There was a lot to learn and even more to tell Corbin about, but when I started the letter to him, I stopped because there was another letter I wanted to write even more.

I changed the address field on the note and started my first letter to the man I'd been calling Dragonfly in my mind since I'd learned what the tattoo on his ribs was.

> *Dear Dragonfly,*
> *I've finished my first week of classes here at the academy. Classes are good. I have three roommates, and they seem nice. They don't bother me at least. I really do love it here and can't wait to become a pilot. You helped me get here. Thank you for that.*
> *Thierry*

I wasn't sure what else to say to him, so I quickly sent the note off before I could think better of writing to him. The thousand credits a month would be amazing, but that wasn't the only reason I was making a note. I wanted to thank him for helping me, and now I had, so I could write a note to Corbin and then go back to studying, like my roommates were on their own beds.

WE WERE off every weekend, and even though we couldn't go off-world, we could leave the academy as long as we were back by Sunday night at eight. Since most of the people there lived on the world already, they went home. Me, I planned to sleep in and stare at the ships all day, which was where I was when Corbin called me just after eleven.

"Hey," I said, putting the earpiece for my com unit into my ear so we could talk.

"Hey, future pilot. What are your plans for today?"

I shrugged and put my arms on the railing, looking out at the atrium where the smallest of the display ships were held. "Nothing too much. I have a free day today. I'll probably get more studying in. There's plenty we're expected to know right away, and my math is a little rusty for the calculations."

Corbin laughed, and I smiled. "Take a day off. Study tomorrow. I saw that the weather is good there. Well, not as good as on Wish, where I am."

"Yeah, it's hard to beat artificially created weather that is perfect all the time." Corbin's being on Wish reminded me of Dragonfly. I'd been a bit disappointed not to get a letter back from him overnight, but then again Monroe had never said that Dragonfly would be writing back. "I got my letter out last night." I wouldn't be saying more than that about it while I was there. Even though there weren't that many people around, I still didn't want anyone to guess what I was talking about.

"Good."

I was glad Corbin had figured out what I was talking about without me having to spell it out for him. "Lots lined up for you today?"

"Of course. Monroe likes to keep us busy. More money for us, and lots for him too. There's even some new ones, though I don't think one of them is going to make it here."

Corbin usually didn't tell me much about his work, but maybe since I'd been there, he felt more comfortable talking about it. Like maybe I wouldn't go screaming for the hills anymore after what I'd done. He was right, I could handle it. And Wish was such a big part of my brother's life, I should have known more about his work a lot sooner than I had.

"Oh?" I asked him. He'd arrived on Wish the night before, which meant the new guy had too. It was hard to believe someone was making trouble already.

I heard people talking in the background and figured he was getting something to eat since it was so close to lunchtime. "He refused to take a client, which isn't something Monroe lets us do. I mean, if someone is mean or treats us badly, then that's fine, Monroe will take care of it. But he just straight out refused because the guy was so much older than him. You should have seen Monroe. He was pissed. Had the guy scrubbing the floors by hand for at least an hour."

"Wow." I could picture how upset Monroe would have been by that. I hadn't seen him mad, but he had looked like he could get really mean if he wanted to, like he had some kind of ice in him, and if pushed too hard, could come out and just make him snap. I shivered, not wanting to think about him anymore. "So what happened?"

"Guy got a refund and a free date. Well, for him it was free. Monroe still paid me for my time."

I shifted my weight. "You don't sound like it bothered you."

"What? His age? No. Older guys don't bother me. Younger don't either. And even though he didn't have to pay for my time, he still tipped me really well. I ended up making more than I would have anyway, after Monroe paid me too. He wasn't a jerk or anything, so I hope he comes back. I wouldn't mind him being a regular."

In a way it was strange talking to Corbin about his work, but another side of it was that now we'd done the same thing, or nearly so. I'd only had one client, and that's all I was ever going to have, but we had both sold ourselves for our futures. Sure, Corbin could have somehow made it work in the mines, but it was a hard life for anyone, especially someone who was nearly an adult having to raise their little brother like a son.

"Thank you for what you did back then, when you first went to work there. I didn't understand, but I think I'm getting it now," I told him solemnly. Maybe, in some strange way, what we'd both done would bring us closer. I loved my brother very much, but we hadn't been all that close, partially because of the age difference, but more because he hadn't been around much when I was growing up. After our parents died in an accident, he'd had to work a lot to keep us both fed.

Corbin chuckled, and I hoped he wasn't going to brush off my sincerity. "You make it sound like a hardship, little brother. Meeting up with Monroe, doing what I do while I'm here on Wish, this is fun for me. I like being around people, I like helping them. I like getting to try new things, and I enjoy being with the people who maybe aren't able to have relationships with others as easily as some do. A lot of the guys who come to me may want easy sex with someone who won't insist on seeing them every night or expect to get a com call the next morning. But there are a lot of people out there too, who don't think they're worthy of love or a relationship in general, so they come to Asiq, and for a little while, they're the center of someone's world. It's a fantasy, and I don't think about them much after they're gone, but I see how a man's face lights up when I address him by name or welcome him back to Asiq, or tell him he's been missed, or I ask about the child he mentioned once in passing, and they just look happy. That's why I do this. The sex is generally good, and I get my needs met while I'm here, but it's the helping people I like most."

I took a deep breath and tried to see it from his perspective, which honestly was a bit hard. Because I didn't see people like Corbin did, and even though I'd now been living with three other guys for the past week, I still couldn't remember their names. I should have probably tried harder to learn them, and I decided I would.

"You really wouldn't leave it, would you?" I asked him.

"No, Thierry, I really wouldn't. Monroe is going to have to kick me out when I'm too old to work, and even then I'll probably beg to stay and work in the kitchen or something. Some people, like you, want to be a pilot. Others are doctors, some are miners, and the list goes on. Me, I like what I do. It's a little weird, and I don't mind if you want to tell your friends I do something else with my time, but it's not a source of shame for me. I'm proud of it."

I licked my lips and started back to my room to relax for a while. It was nice not to have everyone else around during the weekend, and the school became much quieter. "It's not for me either. And I wouldn't lie about what you do. It makes you happy."

"Yes, it does. What are you doing this afternoon?" he asked me as I took the glass elevator upstairs to the men's dorm.

"Not much. Maybe grab something to eat later. I miss chocolate." The elevator opened, and I stepped out into the shiny white and stainless steel hall. They all looked the same, but at least there were signs telling me where I was so if, and more often when, I got lost, I could figure out where I was.

"I'll save you some for when I see you next. I've got a client coming in a little bit who I need to get ready for. You'll be okay?"

I nodded and went into my room to lie down on my bed after kicking off my shoes. "Yeah. See you later."

"Bye."

He hung up, and I took out my earpiece. I figured I could maybe take a nap, even though I'd slept in, or maybe I could read and catch up on what was happening in the universe. But when I took out my holoscreen, I noticed I had a note waiting for me. If it had been from Corbin, he would have mentioned sending it to me, and since no one else wrote me, I was nervous as I opened it. It was from Monroe, but it was a forwarded message, and my heart immediately started racing when I realized it was from Dragonfly.

> *Thierry,*
> *I was glad to get your letter and to hear you made it safely to the academy. I wish you the best of luck in your endeavors and hope my continued support of your goals in life brings you a bit of peace. I was fortunate in my younger years, and I feel a good deal of joy at being able to share what wealth I have amassed with someone like you. You gave me a gift, and I was happy to return the favor.*
> *Yours Always,*
> *Dragonfly*

I smiled down at my holoscreen and I crossed my ankles above my butt and swung them. I had so many questions for him, though I doubted he'd be willing to answer any of them. I wanted to know his name, though I had a feeling that would likely be the last question from me he'd ever answer.

> *Dear Dragonfly,*
> *I'm glad you wrote back. I didn't think you would. Nearly everyone in the academy is gone for the weekend. The teachers are still here, along with the deans, but for the most part, I'm alone here. But I'm not lonely. It's actually fairly nice having everything so quiet.*
> *I have loads of questions for you, though I have a feeling your need for secrecy will make you unable to*

*answer them. Which is okay. I don't want to pressure
you into answering. I'm glad you wrote back at all. I
wasn't expecting that.*

*I guess my first question would be this; where did
your wealth come from?*

I stared at my holoscreen for a long time as I wondered how to sign off. When he'd written *Yours Always,* what had that meant? I didn't even know his real name, so how could he be mine? And I didn't think of myself as his at all. I'd shared something so intimate with him, but I knew nothing about him. It made signing my note back to him hard.

In the end I simply signed with my name, just as I'd done with the first letter, before sending off the note and opening up the magazines I had subscriptions to. A few were science based, one was all about exploration, which I read eagerly, and then there was the one I'd just signed up for, which was a gossip magazine about the celebrities of the universe. It wasn't something I normally read, and I skimmed through it as I looked at the pictures. As silly as it was, I'd signed up for it to search for a picture of a Denobelas man with a tattoo of a dragonfly on his ribs. I knew how bad it would have sounded had anyone actually known my reasons for subscribing. It was crazy and stalkerish. But I wanted to know who Dragonfly was. It was a need inside me I couldn't shake. Maybe if we'd had sex and that had been the end of it, I wouldn't care. But once he'd asked me to write to him, I'd wanted to know more about him.

The magazine gave me no new information, not that I expected it to. I knew finding out his secrets in those digital pages was a long shot. But I wasn't willing to cut the subscription service either as I decided to hold on to that flare of hope for another two weeks until my next magazine came.

The rest of my day was spent being fairly lazy, especially for me, which was saying something since back on the space station, my time had revolved around reading, napping, and eating with very little cleaning when the place needed it or I ran out of clothes to wear. I couldn't sit around naked there while I waited for the steam press to clean my clothes, and I knew I'd have to stay more on top of that than I had back home.

By the time I was ready to go to bed, still alone in the dorm, I'd hardly done more than go downstairs to the cafeteria to grab one of the ready meals that were left for those of us who didn't leave the academy on the weekends. My choices were limited, but I managed to find some pudding and a peanut butter sandwich. I was sure some of my classmates would have objected to the meal, since a lot of them seemed fairly prissy, but it was nice to eat something that didn't have a shelf time of twenty years and come instantly to life after adding boiling water to it, like I'd had on the space station.

I was heading back upstairs when I got another notification of a note waiting for me on my holoscreen. It was probably another spam message. I received them frequently now that I was closer to the inner planets where far more people lived. But it was a note from Dragonfly and I smiled as I started to read it and eat at the same time. My bed was far more comfortable to eat in and I was glad no one had been around to stop me from bringing food upstairs.

> *Dear Thierry,*
>
> *When I was a child much younger than you, I had a grandfather whom I adored. He was wealthier than most people could ever imagine, and I would spend every summer with him. He was my world while my parents were off having their own adventures and traveling the system. He died and left me everything. I was barely a man with far too much money for any one person to have control over, and that it had been left to me and not to my father, his son, was a source of strife between us.*

TO THE HIGHEST BIDDER

I didn't understand why I'd benefited from his death, and I had certainly never asked him to leave it all to me, but my father didn't believe me and thought somehow I had tricked my grandfather, whom I had loved and respected, into naming me his sole heir.

I could no longer live there. I stayed on my grandfather's property for nearly a year, but the memories were too great. Sometimes I felt as if I was suffocating under them.

And so, when I was even younger than you, I set out to find my own way. I made plenty of mistakes in my youth and invested a good deal of that money in ventures that never saw the light of day.

When I saw the advertisement set forth by Asiq, I found you attractive, but more than your physical beauty, I thought yours was a noble choice, to want something so greatly you would be willing to engage in such intimacy for a chance to follow your dreams. I must admit that when I was your age, I had no such sweeping ambitions, and it was that more than anything else which made me bid on you.

I hope I have answered your question thoroughly and you are able to enjoy what is left of your weekend. I imagine this to be a busy time for you. Should you wish to ask me further questions, I will answer them the best that I can. I will not tell you who I am, for I assure you that would be disastrous, but I will be honest with you when I can and share with you what I wish.

Would it be all right with you if I asked you questions from time to time as well, should the desire arise?

Yours Always,
Dragonfly

I ate as I carefully thought about the questions I wanted to ask him. I was still most desperate to know who he was, but I felt lucky to get any insight into his life up to this point. I understood needing to be secretive, since I certainly wasn't sharing with any of the people at the academy that I'd spent time on Wish, but in a way I thought he should be able to share something with me. I mean, we'd done things that people who loved each other did. And it bothered me that I didn't know what he looked like or what his name was.

Thinking about the hours we'd spent together made my body hum a little, and as I reached down to adjust myself, my nerves flared to life even more as I thought about Dragonfly's hand on me and how I'd felt as he'd spilled into me and cried out against my neck.

There was no denying my response now, and since I was alone, I figured I could take a few minutes. My roommates had said they wouldn't be back for the rest of the weekend since they had family things to do, not that I'd asked. It was more like we were all sitting around and they'd asked me what my plans for the weekend were. I hadn't had any, of course, and they'd given me a look of pity.

It didn't matter anyway. What did matter was that I could get up and go lock the door. I had to be fast, just in case, and also quiet too. I hadn't thought about Dragonfly like that since our time together, but as I undid the drawstring on my pants and pulled my shirt up to keep it from getting dirty, I couldn't have said why I hadn't thought about him. Our time together had been pleasurable, and maybe he thought about me like that too. Maybe he lay awake at night, stroking himself like I was doing now as I thought about him on top of me, his smooth body sliding against mine as he filled me, his mouth covering mine. It wasn't long before I was gritting my teeth and covering my mouth as I jerked in pleasure. I cleaned myself up quickly, then unlocked the door before sitting down on my bed. I was still panting a little, and as I opened up my notes to write back to Dragonfly, I momentarily considered telling him about what I'd just done. But then I thought better of it.

> *Dear Dragonfly,*
> *You may ask me anything you want. I won't hide*
> *stuff from you. Thank you for telling me a bit about*
> *yourself. Did you ever fix things with your dad?*
> *Thierry*

With my note sent off, and feeling like I was suddenly on fire, I knew it would be a long time before I went to bed that night as I waited patiently for my next letter from the man I knew as Dragonfly.

CHAPTER SEVEN

TWO WEEKS later I hadn't learned much more about Dragonfly than I'd started with. He evaded each of my questions or simply told me the answer wasn't pertinent, like his personal life wasn't something I needed to know. It was in those moments of frustration that I reminded myself of the basis of our relationship, if it could even be called that, and that reality was often a hard pill for me to swallow.

The first time we were allowed to go off-world happened pretty uneventfully. People took vacations to the terraformed tropical moon that was only a short day trip away, or used the jump gates in space to go farther. I planned to spend the weekend like I had each one since getting to the academy: in my bed, relaxing with my holoscreen while I waited to either talk to Corbin or receive a note from Dragonfly.

So when my com beeped, letting me know I had a call waiting, I figured it was Corbin. "Hey," I said as I put the earpiece into my ear and got more comfortable on the ridiculously narrow bed.

"Good morning, Thierry, I trust your Saturday is going well?"

I was surprised to hear from Monroe and wondered what was going on. "Is Corbin okay? Is that why you're calling me?" I demanded as I sat up.

"Your brother is fine. He's with a client right now actually. That's not the reason I'm calling. Do you have plans for the weekend?"

"No." A lot of the people I went to school with did, since there always seemed to be something happening on the nearby moons, but I was never invited. And even if I had been, I probably wouldn't have gone. Most of my free time was spent studying.

"Would you be interested in seeing your client again? He is prepared to offer you five thousand for your time tonight. Same expectations as before. You will be fed and secrecy will be maintained, even with the other men at Asiq."

Of course I wanted to come back and see Dragonfly. Monroe should have led with that instead of making me worry. "I don't have a way to get off-world, and all the shuttles left shortly before dawn this morning. There aren't even any transport ships coming until after the weekend."

"I will schedule one for you. Be at the shuttle bay in an hour. You'll take a shuttle to the jump gate, where a transporter will take you to your home space station. You'll have half an hour to stop by your home, if you need anything, and from there you'll take another short-range shuttle to Wish. You'll be here by three."

It took me a minute to get over his rapid planning. "Wow, you're thorough."

"I'm also busy, as I'm sure I don't need to remind you. Can I expect you at the shuttle port in an hour?"

"I'm leaving now." I started getting the things I'd need together. I had to let the deans know I was going off-world for the weekend, but I accomplished that easily with a quick note to them. We weren't required to tell them where we were going or who we'd be with, but they did need to know we'd be gone in case we didn't make it back by Sunday night. No one had missed check-in yet, and I didn't want to be the first to make that mistake.

"Good. I will let him know you've agreed." He sounded pleased, and I was sure that meant he was getting a lot of money out of my meeting with Dragonfly. Knowing that didn't bother me one bit. I only cared about seeing Dragonfly again.

I looked around to make sure there was nothing else I needed. I didn't think there was, and if I forgot something it wasn't as if Monroe wasn't well stocked at Asiq for most of what I'd need there.

"What's your cut this time?" It was a fair question since he was a businessman and would be getting something for his time.

He chuckled, and I finished sending the note to the deans and the last of my packing. "The five thousand is after my cut. Do you have any other questions?"

"No." I couldn't believe Dragonfly was offering that much to spend a few hours with me. I also couldn't get over seeing Dragonfly again. I was nearly running when I left the dorm with a bag in my hands. "Good. Then I expect you to be on time. If, for some reason, you will be late, I expect a call."

I would be on time, as long as nothing happened between shuttles and jumps. But he didn't need to remind me to call him as if I was irresponsible. I wasn't one of his aspasians, but I wasn't a child either, and not much could stop me from seeing Dragonfly again as far as I was concerned. "Of course. I've leaving for the shuttles now. Bye."

I ran down the stairs. I could have gone slower. I probably could have even taken my time, but I was too anxious to see Dragonfly again, which was silly because I hardly even knew him, but I was also crossing systems, and it would take hours to get to Wish.

"Bye," Monroe told me.

I was hailing a hovercab before he finished hanging up. The shuttle station was busy, but I managed to find my platform and squeeze in between two people waiting to go off-world just like I was. Monroe had arranged everything, and the short ride to the jump gate was crowded, but I didn't worry about it since I wouldn't be on it long.

"Are you at the academy?" the woman next to me asked as I got comfortable in my seat and strapped myself in. She had beautiful iridescent feathers going down her neck like a collar. I didn't know what she was and knew better than to be rude by asking. Since we were headed toward a jump gate that would take us all over the universe, she could have been from anywhere. Seeing her made me want to explore new places even more once I became a pilot.

It took me a moment to figure out why she was asking me that until I realized I still had my uniform jacket on, with its bright crest that let everyone know I was from the academy. I was glad I'd brought it since the shuttle was a bit chilly.

"Yes, I am."

"What would you like to be when you're done?" she continued. I figured small talk must be what people on shuttles did to pass time. We were nearing the moon, and I glanced out the windows beside me to look at its pale pink surface. Gasses, I'd learned, made it that color.

"A pilot," I answered automatically. I hadn't ever wanted to be anything else. "Intersystem," I clarified, in case she thought I wanted to pilot short-range shuttles like this the rest of my life, which honestly, wasn't a bad deal. But I wanted to see new worlds, and I couldn't do that, being in a single system.

She gave me a dry little chuckle, and I turned to look back at her, wondering why that was funny. "I take this shuttle all the time when I visit my family on the weekends, and I ask all of you students the exact same question. You're the first not to tell me you've got your heart set on being the captain of some big cruiser. It's refreshing."

I smiled at her. "Thank you." I could never be a captain, but I did know what she was talking about since I'd seen the same thing with my classmates. They wanted to be the ones giving orders from some coveted chair. I just wanted to fly through space.

There was a jolt as the ship docked at the jump gate, and she patted my shoulder once we were allowed to get up. "Have a good time off-world," she called as she got off the crowded shuttle.

"You too," I told her. I grabbed my bag and headed out as well.

I'd been to the jump gate before, but I'd never seen it so busy, and I nearly got lost trying to find the transport ship Monroe had booked me on. As it was, I nearly missed it while I was trying to find something that was right in front of my face.

Being on a transport ship was a lot different than being on a shuttle, because it was so much bigger and they went not just between worlds but between star systems and explored the entire universe. That's the kind of pilot I wanted to be, and I listened to the pilots talking with a good bit of envy after I knelt to put my bag in the cargo compartment below my seat then strapped myself in.

I knew this ride would take longer than the shuttle, so I tried to relax even as I could hardly hold still in my excitement to see Dragonfly again. We approached the jump gate, and my anticipation of seeing him combined with my desire to go pilot through a jump gate on my own made me excited and nearly unable to sit still. Only trained pilots were allowed to use them, and we had to wait our turn as people going to other systems were allowed to go first. I was nearly bouncing when the captain spoke over the internal com unit to let us know we were next.

To me, going through a wormhole created by a jump gate didn't feel any different than any other time I went through space, despite how much I'd hoped it would. As a child the idea of going through a wormhole and getting sucked from one part of space to another sounded incredibly scary and wonderful. Now that I'd done it a few times, it wasn't as scary but it was amazing. I thought about how all of space worked together and how long it must have taken the first of us to be able to go through space. No wonder new systems weren't discovered for centuries after people first started leaving their home worlds.

It only took about an hour to get to my home system and, as we docked at the space station that was the central hub of the planet, it felt good to be back in familiar territory. From there, I took a smaller shuttle I thought was going to take me to Wish, but the driver brought me back to my little space station.

"Aren't we going to Wish?" I asked him as he docked outside our apartment like Corbin always did.

He shook his head. "Mr. Monroe wanted you to have half an hour to get anything you needed from here first. My instructions are to wait for you. If you're late, though, I can leave."

I'd completely forgotten about the time Monroe had given me at home. I didn't need a lot, since most of my things were at the academy, but it would still feel good to be home for a few minutes, even if I didn't do anything while I was there.

"Thanks. I'll be back on time."

"Thirty minutes," he reminded me once the air lock opened and I was allowed to leave the two-person shuttle.

I went inside the apartment. People weren't allowed to stay docked outside for long, which was probably why Monroe had put a thirty-minute cap on my time inside. After that time, shuttles were pulled into the shuttle bay so the station wasn't covered with small shuttles blocking people from coming home.

Once inside my plan of relaxing on the couch went out the window. I had plenty of clothes at the academy, but it was good to have more. And I would probably need an extra charger for my holoscreen too, and another comb was probably a good idea.

By the time I finished shoving things into my bag, I was nearly out of time. I hurried back to the shuttle in case the driver decided to get impatient and leave me. Thankfully he was still there, and I put my things away and got settled for the long flight to Wish.

It was nearly three in the afternoon by the time I stepped into Asiq. I had decided to come in the front door and smiled at the guy, who wasn't much older than me, manning the large desk.

"Hello, sir. Welcome to Asiq. Are you an expected guest, or would you like to make an appointment? To your left you'll find holocards of all our currently available men. Any of them would be happy to attend to your needs this afternoon."

It sounded so rehearsed and yet completely genuine coming from him, but I realized I probably should have come in the back way instead so that no one saw me. "Uh. I'm here to see Monroe. Can you let him know Thierry is here?"

The man's silver, scale-covered face dipped a little in a frown. "Monroe isn't one of the people available for an appointment. Please choose one of the men from the left."

I shifted the bag on my shoulder and wished I hadn't overfilled it with things at the apartment. "I'm not here for that," I told him a bit impatiently. "I'm here to see Monroe."

"But—"

"Hey, you're Corbin's brother, aren't you?"

I turned, hoping it wasn't a client. I couldn't tell if the man looking at me from the bar in the corner was or not. It wasn't like they all wore big signs or anything.

I nodded and waved at him. "Hi. Yeah, I'm his brother. Thierry."

The guy at the bar nodded. "Darcelen, let the kid in. He's here to see his brother."

"Rex, he said he wanted to see Monroe, who you know is busy," Darcelen told him.

Rex rolled his eyes and pointed with a pink drink in the direction of a pale green painted hallway just to my left, past the screen of advertised, available men. "Go down there. He's in room twelve. Best to let Monroe know you're here first."

"I was trying to." That came out meaner than I'd intended, and maybe I should have explained things to Darcelen first, but I was tired and really needed to get cleaned up before I saw Dragonfly again.

Darcelen blushed and tilted his head to the side. "I apologize for the confusion. Of course you may go back and find Monroe now. He should be in his office. Please let him know you've arrived before visiting your brother."

I nodded, then came to my senses. "I'm sorry I didn't explain better the first time. It's been a long day."

Darcelen smiled, though he did look surprised by my apology. "That's understandable. You've come from the academy by the looks of your jacket. It's a long way to travel. Please enjoy your stay on Wish."

"Will do. Thanks."

I gave them both a little wave before going to find Monroe's office. I knocked and was glad I didn't have to wait long before I was called to enter.

"Hi," I said as I came in and closed the door quietly behind me.

He looked up from his desk and put the holoscreen in his hands aside. "I take it your trip was uneventful?" I nodded. "Good. Put your things in the same room as last time, next to your brother's. You have an hour to spend with him before you meet your client."

"Dragonfly," I said, bristling.

Monroe frowned. "I beg your pardon?"

I licked my lips and wished the academy weren't so far away from Wish. I'd been hardy able to sit still on the shuttles over, and now I felt nearly drained of energy. Whenever I was tired, my mouth tended to get away from me sometimes. I had to work on that before I met with Dragonfly. I didn't want to upset him.

Monroe looked at me as if I'd gone crazy. "Are you clear on your instructions?"

I nodded and started toward the door. "Put my stuff down, I get an hour, then gotta get ready. Simple."

"One last thing before you go, Thierry," he called, stopping me.

I turned, one hand already on the door. "Yes?"

He got up from the desk, and I wondered what was going on now. "I'll be running another test. The vaccine keeps you from getting any diseases and hanging on to them, but if you've been with an infected person in the last forty-eight hours, you could still give something to someone else. You can stand. No reason to have you sitting down for this again. This is the normal routine everyone goes through, though my men get this done in their rooms electronically. You haven't been shown how to use the machine, so I'll be doing it for you."

"Why explain it? Why not just tell me you need to do the test?" I asked. I clamped down hard on my nerves as he lifted my shirt and pressed a shiny silver disk against my skin. It hurt, just as before, and I cried out a little.

When I swayed forward, Monroe put his hand squarely in the center of my chest, keeping me upright. I shut my eyes and tried not to feel the pain pulsing through my arm. If I opened myself, the heat would have overridden the pain, and it would have been far more bearable. But I only opened myself up for Dragonfly now.

"Because, Thierry, even though you do sell yourself like my men, you are not one of them, and I don't need you upset and unable to get out of your own head with your cli—Dragonfly around."

I was glad he'd changed what he was going to say at the last minute. That mattered to me. The test was over, and he stepped back, letting me go.

"I could have told you I haven't been with anyone since I was here last," I said. I shouldn't have been annoyed at him, but I was.

Monroe lifted his dark eyebrows and looked at the disk. "I wouldn't have believed you." The disk beeped.

I was a bit surprised by that. Didn't he trust anyone? "Because you think I'd lie to you?"

Monroe laughed, and I scowled when I realized he was actually laughing at me. "It doesn't matter if you'd lie to me. I'm fairly certain boys your age lie to everyone at some point. No, Thierry, the reason I wouldn't have believed you is because you are a twenty-year-old young man who has recently had his eyes opened to the wonderful world of sex, with lots of opportunity and time available should you wish to indulge yourself. Most of my men don't go a day without sex when they're outside. I don't expect you to be any different and you've been gone a month."

I knew what he was saying, but he was wrong about me. "Would it have made a difference if I'd told you that I hardly ever even thought about sex while I was gone?"

He shook his head, and I shrugged, not knowing why I had bothered. If Monroe thought I was having sex with everyone in my dorm, it wouldn't have mattered anyway. And, as I thought about what he'd said, he probably thought I was screwing everyone in the academy.

"Can I go hang out with Corbin now?"

Monroe nodded. "You may. Do you remember how to get back to the room with the red door?"

I would always know how to get there. My time with Dragonfly had been just that important to me. "Yes."

"Good. Then I expect you to be there by four. You'll have an hour to prepare, as usual, and dinner will be served again. Let no one know what you're doing here. Corbin has an appointment in an hour, so that will give you an excuse to leave him for the evening. Now go on. I'm busy."

I smiled at that, since Monroe always seemed to be in a hurry to let people know he was busy, then headed to the room next to my brother's. I dropped my stuff off, left my jacket on, then went next door to knock on Corbin's door.

"Thierry? What are you doing here?" He sounded surprised, probably because I hadn't let him know I was coming to Asiq. It was so good to hug him, though, as we grabbed each other tightly.

We went into my room because it was clean and flopped down on the bed together since there was nowhere to sit and talk.

"I came to see you," I told him. It was only half a lie, since I had wanted to see him too. "It's my one weekend a month off-world."

Corbin nodded. "I remember. How'd you manage it?"

"I used some of the credits I'm getting paid to write the guy letters." It was a lie, and I tried to keep it nonchalant. I could have told him Monroe had paid for my trip, but I didn't think Corbin would believe he'd done that without expecting something out of me in return. And he would have been right.

So the lie was better, and Corbin seemed to believe it. "How's that going? Is he weird or anything like that to you? I don't want you feeling uncomfortable or like you have to write to him or something like that."

I instantly shook my head. "He's fine. We talk about my classes and things like that. Nothing personal about him at all, or me either, really." I wasn't sure why I felt defensive on Dragonfly's behalf, but I did. I wished I knew more about him, or had something to tell him outside of how my classes were going. But if my classmates had anything to share, any tidbits of juicy gossip that I could have shared with Dragonfly, they certainly didn't tell me. I felt like I'd been at the academy for a while now, but I was still the outsider that no one wanted to sit near or talk to. It was lonely, but getting to talk to Corbin all the time helped, just like writing to Dragonfly did.

"That's good. Sometimes I worry about you talking to him. Seems kind of creepy."

"It's not, though. He's nice." Corbin dropped it, and I didn't try to convince him anymore. I knew how it looked from the outside, which was fine. Corbin wasn't involved so of course he wouldn't know that Dragonfly's letters to me were always really polite. He'd never once been rude or crass to me, and I knew he respected me.

Corbin and I hung out and talked about classes until it was time for him to go. I waited a few minutes to make sure he didn't see me take off down the hallway before I left too. My heart was racing as I went into the room and washed, brushed my teeth, then got dressed in the robe again, like Dragonfly wanted me to.

When I came out of the bathroom, there was only one plate of food. I figured we'd be sharing, which wasn't super weird, I guessed. When the door opened and Dragonfly came in wearing an expensive looking dark blue shirt, black slacks, and shiny black shoes, along with the same mask as before, I smiled at him.

And he smiled back, which made me smile even more. He closed the door behind him and instead of sitting down to eat, like I had the first time, I went up to him like he was a friend of mine, which in a way he'd started to become after talking to him in letters for so many weeks. I put my fingertips on his stomach and tilted my head back for a kiss.

Thankfully he let me have that kiss, and I opened up for him as he pressed his tongue against my lips and heat traveled along my spine where he held me. He put his hands on the knot of my robe, and I froze a little before I let him open it, then slide the thin material off my shoulders. It was the same as the first time we'd been together, and the familiarity and ritual of it helped me relax.

I hadn't been scared in that moment, and I hoped he didn't think I was either, but I had been surprised he wanted me naked already. I'd been so looking forward to seeing him, I'd forgotten about the pain that had come with my first time or how nervous I'd felt in front of him. He kissed me again, and I was sure we'd go to the bed next as he ran his hands down my sides and over my arms.

But instead he led me over to the table, where he sat down to dinner. He didn't let go of my hand so I could sit down, and for a moment, I wasn't sure what he wanted me to do. Then he pointed at the floor by his feet, and even though it felt a little strange sitting next to someone while they ate, I still did it. I played with my fingernails while he poured himself a glass of wine and ate the sliced meat laid out on a platter for us to share.

It was strange being beside him and not doing anything. I had no idea what I was supposed to be doing, and it didn't help that he wasn't talking to me, as usual. Sometimes I wondered if he even could talk, or if something had happened to him to take that ability away. I wish I knew.

"The trip over from the academy was good. I met a lady on the first shuttle who was surprised I wanted to be a pilot. She said most people from the academy wanted to be captains. I couldn't do that. I only want to fly."

He put a piece of meat in front of me, and I reached up to take it, but when I lifted my hand, he pulled it away from me. He put a little pressure on the back of my head, and it came to me he wanted me to eat from his hand. As strange things went, this wasn't all that bad. And after the piece of meat I ate off his fingers, he brought the wineglass to my lips and gave me a little drink. Cheese came next, and soon I was eating small bites as often as he was until I looked over the edge of the table and saw the plate was nearly empty and the wine was gone. I was a bit disappointed that he was done feeding me, but I was full too.

He turned sideways on his chair, and I backed up a little, giving him more room to get up. But instead of standing, he started to undo his pants. I might have been new to sex, but I knew what he was doing, so when he took himself out, I was right there waiting for him. I closed my eyes and brought my lips around his head, and when he put one hand on the back of my hair, I didn't struggle. He tasted as good as ever, and I took my time enjoying him. Resting my hands on his thighs felt natural and right. Without him telling me what to do, I was able to figure that out for myself.

I only got a few minutes before he pulled back and stood. He stripped off his clothes, and when he was naked in front of me, I traced the dragonfly tattoo on his ribs for a moment before he put his hand over mine, then curled his fingers around them and helped me to my feet. He led me over to the bed, and I smiled as I anticipated what was about to happen between us.

But when we got there, and I put a knee on the bed, getting ready to lie down on my back for him again, he turned me over so I was on my stomach. He helped me get my knees under me, then ran a hand down my back, right over my spine. I was still open to him, and I gasped as he touched me, even though it was the lightest of touches. I turned to look at him, completely unsure of myself as he went over to the basket beside the bed and opened some lubricant. I bit my bottom lip as he began to stretch me as carefully as he had before. I wished I could see more of his face.

He was smiling a little, and I smiled back at him, even though I was nervous.

I wished he would have said something to calm my nerves, but I knew he wouldn't. I took a deep breath and cried out when he put a hand on either side of my hips and pulled me back to meet him. I let my forehead fall onto the bed and whimpered as I opened up as much as I could, which let me feel everything much more intensely.

He'd been good to me before, but I realized he'd been going easy on me and being gentle because it had been my first time. When he was inside me, I was shaking and sore enough that I knew I'd be feeling him for at least a few days, if not a week. Pulling out of me, he turned me over and kissed me hard. I wrapped my legs around his waist and put my hands on his shoulders, ready for more.

He pushed into me, making me arch off the bed, and I moaned as he wrapped a hand around my shaft, making me come as before. I was exhausted when he got up after finishing inside of me, and though I expected him to clean me like he had before, this time he lifted me into his arms and put me over his shoulder, before taking me into the bathroom and placing me into the large tub. I wanted him to join me in the bath he started for me, but he didn't. Instead he knelt beside the tub and held my hand under the water. The tub was plenty big enough for both of us, and I was disappointed that he hadn't wanted to come wash off with me.

"Thank you," I mumbled. I was sore, and it felt like I'd been stretched everywhere. But I also felt alive and wonderful in a way I was coming to know with him. He kissed me, and I put my hand on the back of his neck, hoping to keep him close, but he broke away. He left me lying there in the tub with the hot water running over my legs and the door open so I could see him as he got dressed and then left me as silently as he'd arrived.

That night while I was getting ready to return to the academy, I received a note from him that simply said, *You're welcome.*

CHAPTER EIGHT

A WEEK later I had a few minutes before my next class, so I pulled out my holoscreen as I leaned against a wall in the atrium. There weren't any notes I hadn't already read, and most of those had been Corbin teasing me about the chocolate he knew I missed. He'd even sent me vids of the tiny treats being unwrapped, like a jerk.

Instead of sending him a note to pass the time, I decided to write to Dragonfly.

Dear Dragonfly, I began, wishing once again I knew his name. I scratched that out and started again. *Hey.* It was informal, and maybe we weren't there yet. In fact, we probably weren't. But after writing letters to each other for over a month and being with him twice, I couldn't bring myself to be formal with him as I stared down at my holoscreen. So that was how I chose to start my next note to him.

> *It's always so sunny here, just like on Wish. It barely rains, and after living on the space station for so long, I think I've forgotten what snow feels like. On my home planet, it used to snow all the time. I don't remember it like that, but my brother Corbin used to tell me about it. He says children used to play in the snow and weren't afraid of the cold. I guess being in space makes people a lot more worried about the cold*

than they used to be, since it usually means there's a system malfunction or something like that.

I remember this one time when we didn't have life support on the station for a whole two minutes. It might not seem like a lot of time unless you've lived on a station. We all have backup oxygen tanks in case something does happen, but it was still a scary few moments.

I wish I knew your name or what you looked like. I think about you when I'm here. Sometimes I lay awake at night after my roommates have gone to bed and picture you with me. I want to be able to hold your hand, go to the market on Wish, share special times like that with you.

I know we aren't like that, though, that what we have isn't a relationship. But sometimes I let myself daydream that it is, and thinking about you like that makes me smile.

I should probably get back to class. I only had a few minutes to spare. Combat training is next. We've read the basics, studied body mechanics, and we'll have padding on, but I'm still worried about getting hurt. I'm smaller than most of the guys in the group, and we know not to take it easy on each other. I really hope I don't end up black and blue in addition to purple by the end of it.

I considered how I was going to end the note. I knew what I wanted to say, what my heart felt, but I didn't know if that was okay to say or not. Screw it, I decided. I would sign it exactly how I wanted to. It was the truth, even if some people might have thought it was fast. I didn't. Not at all.

I love you.
Thierry

There. It was done. I sent it off and stuffed my holoscreen in my bag, hurrying to class so I wouldn't be late. When that happened, the automatic doors refused to open, and I'd receive a failing grade for that day in the class. It was a tough system, but it kept me on time, something I'd never been all that great at.

I was nearly the last one through the door into the large room we were using to practice. I was nervous as I looked around at the group. The girls weren't there since we did everything separately, but I knew from overhearing some of them in the hallways they had combat training that day too.

When I came in, I was already shut down as far as my nerves went. I tried to be like that whenever I was awake now. It was easier that way. The only time I ever really felt anything physical more than a touch or when I ran into something was when I was with Dragonfly. My choice made our time together even more special to me. We Sythe apparently had a reputation, though I hadn't really noticed it before coming here and having to be in tight spaces with other people, and they didn't like coming close enough to me to even risk touching me. It wasn't like I got aroused whenever anyone touched me, but it was difficult sometimes when a little touch resulted in a lot more of a reaction than people typically brought on.

I wasn't looking forward to this lesson at all, but in the end I found myself with the teacher since we were supposed to pair off and, big surprise, no one wanted to be with the highly reactionary Sythe. I rolled my eyes, tried to brush it off, and approached the teacher. Mr. Allessan was a decent guy, I guessed. I mean, I didn't have many classes with him, just the physical stuff. But when it came to actually taking me down in our simulated combat, he didn't hesitate. And it still hurt, despite the pads I was wearing.

I grunted when he landed on top of me, then barely kept my balance when he tried to trip me and failed.

"Good job, Thierry. Work on your balance and overcoming your hesitation to hit someone else before the next class," he told me before he gathered us all back together.

I nodded and said, "Thank you."

At the end of the class, I wasn't any better equipped to handle a hand-to-hand combat situation, but since it was only the first class in that subject, I figured I'd get better at it eventually.

I was sore as I headed back to the dorms, showered, and then lay down in my bed to rest up over my free period. I needed a nap, though I wouldn't have enough time to really get a good one. I was nearly asleep when my holoscreen beeped, and I saw I had a note waiting. My heart started racing when I saw that it was from Dragonfly.

> *Thierry,*
>
> *I shouldn't tell you this, but I love you too, though you'll never hear me say it. Tell them not to hit your face in your combat classes. I like your face. I like all of you, but I would most prefer to see your face stay unblemished.*
>
> *I don't get many days to relax, so I am taking the rare moment to myself to think about you as well. You should know you are never far from my thoughts, and I look forward to the next time I can see you.*
>
> *Yours always,*
> *Dragonfly*

I smiled as I lay down on my pillow. He loved me too. It seemed too unreal to believe, like it was some kind of fantasy. My first time being in love was with someone that loved me too. He was gentle and kind to me. The details of how we'd met, that I didn't know what he looked like or what his voice was like—none of that mattered to me. It was enough that he loved me too.

Three weeks went by quickly, partially because I was busy with my classes, but mostly because I couldn't stop counting down the days until I hopefully got to see Dragonfly again. I was waiting for Monroe's call when it came in Friday night.

"Hi!" I nearly shouted at him once I had the earpiece in my ear.

"Thierry? Are you all right?"

My bright smile lost some of its charm as I forced myself to act like a calm and reasonably mature adult, like I wanted Dragonfly to think of me as. "Yes, I'm fine. Why are you calling?"

"Dragonfly wishes to see you again tomorrow night—if you're willing and have some free time, of course. Your pay would be the same as last time. What answer would you like me to give him?"

"Tell him yes, please." I was bouncing on my bed and attracting the attention of my roommates, so I tried to calm down some more. I really didn't want them asking who I was talking to or why I was so excited.

"Very well. Same routine as last time. Be at the shuttle early. You'll have about an hour again before your appointment."

"Okay. Bye."

"Bye."

He hung up, and I took the earpiece out of my ear. It always kind of hurt a little to have that bud in.

"Girlfriend?" Quatar, one of my roommates, asked as he looked up at me from where he was lying on his bed.

It was easy to shake my head. "Just going to see my brother tomorrow." It wasn't a complete lie.

He nodded. "You must be close."

"We are."

I brought out my holoscreen, and he went back to ignoring me, which was nice since it let me focus on what I'd be doing in less than twenty-four hours. Or, I realized with a grin, whom I'd be doing.

THE NEXT afternoon I was back on Wish and relaxing in Asiq while I counted down the minutes until I got to see Dragonfly again.

"How's classes?" Corbin asked as we split a big pile of chocolates between us on his bed. I'd been through the test again, but this time it hadn't hurt as much. And Monroe hadn't had to stop me from falling forward.

I shrugged. "Decent, I guess. Combat is hard, but I really like learning about the different systems. It's actually a lot tougher than I thought because no one wants to partner with me."

Corbin laughed and popped another chocolate in his mouth. I did the same. "They don't want to turn you on and make you jump them in front of everyone. Sad but true."

I blanched and quickly shook my head. "I wouldn't. I mean, I've got lots of control, but even you wouldn't just randomly have sex with someone in front of other people because they touched you."

Corbin bit his lip, and I stared at him. "You wouldn't...."

His smile broke through, and I knew he'd been playing. "No, of course not. I do have some control, just like you. But I don't clamp down on myself the way you do. There's no reason to when I'm here and people want to see me blush and sigh after just a handshake. Though, speaking of having sex with people, I was with Monroe the other day. It was kind of kinky being with my boss, and he's not half bad, if you're interested."

I rolled my eyes. "Nope. Definitely not." Dragonfly was the only person I was interested in, and Monroe couldn't even start to compare. He was too much of a jerk, too pushy, just plain too bossy for me. It was time for Corbin to go to his next client, and I tried to hide my smile. "See you later," I told him as he started to get up.

"I hate to have to work while you're here. You aren't too bored while I'm gone?"

I would be anything but bored for the next few hours. "I'm good. I promise."

He nodded, and we left the room. "Okay. I'll see you in a little while."

"Yep. See you then."

He started down the hall, and I waited until he went around the corner and couldn't see me anymore before I took off in the opposite direction. I rushed into the room with the red door and stripped off my clothes as quickly as I could. I didn't have to be in such a hurry, but I didn't want to be out of breath when Dragonfly came in either.

I didn't get nearly as much time as I'd thought, not that I was really complaining, because as I was finishing up in the shower, I felt an arm around my stomach pull me out of it. The door had locked automatically behind me, but that didn't mean that Monroe hadn't made a mistake and allowed someone beside myself and Dragonfly to have access to the room. And I'd never thought that Dragonfly would grab me as whoever it was had done.

"Hey!" I shouted, but he put his hand over my mouth, and I struggled until he turned me so I faced the mirror. A second later, once I knew who was holding me, I smiled at Dragonfly, who stood beside me. I liked seeing us together in the mirror, and maybe he did too, because he didn't try to turn me around to face him just yet.

He put a hand under my chin and turned my head to the side so he could kiss me while also brushing a hand down my stomach to cup me. I flared open for him and sighed when he released my mouth.

"This is a good surprise," I told him as I reached up to rest my hands on either side of his neck. I was quickly getting hard for him as he teased me, and I thought he would take me in the bathroom, something I had spent a bit of time fantasizing about, but he let go of me to walk me toward the bed. We lay down together, with him behind me, and he slid an arm under my head while taking me in his hand again.

I smiled and put one of my legs over his and then reached back to touch his hip. "I missed you." He kissed the back of my head, and I figured that might mean he had too.

I felt him getting hard against my ass, and he gently readied me for him before pushing inside me again. I trembled as we lay together and he thrust into me. I had enjoyed each time with him, but this one was the most gentle, and the slowest.

Once he'd figured out a rhythm that worked for both of us, he teased my nipples—something I discovered I liked—playing with them before moving back to my cock.

I whimpered, and he bit the back of my shoulder as I sprayed the sheets and his hand a few minutes later. He wasn't far behind me, and once he finished, I figured it was time to get up, but he didn't let me. He kept me there, holding me as my racing heart slowed to normal.

"I love you," I whispered. I closed my eyes, realizing he wouldn't say it back to me, and not wanting him to see I was disappointed by that.

He turned me over in his arms and kissed me. I wrapped my legs around him and rested my hands on his shoulders as he lay on top of me. He was bigger than me, and I guessed by the way he spoke about his past and how he talked in general, he was older too.

"Tell me something about yourself when you send me your next note please," I told him. I realized there was no question of whether or not I would be getting another note from him, only when it would come. I expected to return to Asiq on the last Saturday of the month, and I expected to have notes from him often.

It was a strange relationship, and one I wouldn't have chosen for myself at all, but to me it was real. It felt real, and I knew nothing else, and that was all that mattered. I only hoped he felt the same way. He'd told me he loved me, so he must. I was sure of it. I was his and he was mine.

He kissed me again before going down my body with his warm tongue and gentle kisses. When he closed his mouth around my soft head, I gasped and propped myself up on my elbows to be able to watch him. I wasn't ready right away, but with him working his mouth over me, it didn't take me all that long to get there.

I bit my bottom lip and nearly fell backward as I spilled into his mouth. I hadn't expected him to do that for me, and when he pulled away and took my hand, I came toward him. "Don't you want me to?" I asked him when he got up and stepped out of my reach.

He shook his head, and I was disappointed for a moment, but he brought me over to the table, and we sat down to eat. I was happy and relaxed as I snacked on a selection of cheeses and fruits. No meat this time, but there were some delicious little pastries for us that I devoured even faster than I usually inhaled the chocolates around Asiq.

We were both still naked when, after the plates were empty, he took my hand again and went over to a little music system. A few button touches later, and soft music was playing through the speakers in the wall. I didn't know what language the singer was using, but it didn't really matter as Dragonfly came up behind me and wrapped his arms around my waist. I put my hands over his on my stomach and leaned my head back against his shoulder. He kissed me, and we swayed to the music I couldn't understand but instantly loved, just because he'd chosen it, and we were in this moment together.

He spun me around, and we kissed some more as he reached down to cup my butt. I smiled and swayed with him, putting my hands behind his neck as we kissed. I loved that moment with him and wished it didn't have to end.

But just like every other time, he left me after only a few hours. He waited until I was dressed this time at least. I put my academy jacket on last, and he ran his fingertips down the front of it, right over the academy's emblem of a brightly burning sun.

"It's because they only take the brightest minds," I told him. I put my hand over his when he touched the emblem. It put his hand right over my heart.

He stepped forward to kiss my cheek.

"You don't have to go," I told him, even though I knew I didn't make the decisions here. I just didn't want him to leave me so soon.

His smile looked a little sad before he kissed me again. When he stepped away, I let him go, even though I didn't want to. He gave me a little wave, and then I sat down on the floor in the middle of the room to wait for Monroe to come get me. I didn't care about the mess of the sheets, or the towels in the bathroom, or any of that. I wasn't embarrassed by what I'd done with Dragonfly and I figured Monroe wouldn't care either. That's why we were there after all, to spend time together.

"You look downright pathetic, sitting there like a lost child," Monroe told me as he came in without knocking nearly an hour later.

I shrugged and got to my feet. "Corbin done with his client?"

"Yes. Before you go, I have a present for you from Dragonfly." He pulled a black silicone bracelet out of his pocket and handed it to me.

"What is it?" I asked him, even as I slid it over my left wrist. Whatever it was didn't matter, because it was from Dragonfly, and I'd gladly wear anything he wanted to give me.

Monroe shook his head. "It could have been dangerous. You should have been more careful putting it on."

I rolled my eyes and stuffed my hands into the pockets of my black pants. They'd been bought with the money Dragonfly gave me, and I thought they looked good on me. I realized I should have asked him what he thought of them, but that might have come across as me being vain instead of curious about what he thought of my new clothes. I didn't get new things all that often so I thought it was pretty special to have some new clothes that I'd worn especially for him.

"Dragonfly wouldn't give me anything that could hurt me. He loves me."

Monroe didn't say anything to that.

"And you wouldn't, either," I continued, knowing Monroe would never hurt someone that made him money.

He laughed at that. "Don't delude yourself into thinking I care about you. Kid, you put far too much trust in people for your own good."

"No, of course you don't. But you still wouldn't give me something that could hurt me. Not knowingly anyway." I was sure about that.

"And why do you think that?" Monroe asked.

"Because I make you too much money for you to damage me in any way." I wasn't stupid. I knew where I stood with him. And I knew what he got out of having me there once a month. I brought in money for him, and he didn't have to do much work for it. Just because that was the arrangement between myself and Dragonfly, that didn't make any difference to me where Dragonfly was concerned. I knew he wanted to spend time with me for more than simply sex, though I highly doubted Monroe would see it that way. So I didn't try explaining it to him. It wasn't his business anyway how Dragonfly and I felt about each other.

Monroe smirked and gave me a nod. "This is true. You do make me quite a bit of money, all things considered. Now, back to your bracelet. It's got a tracker in it, and it has a microphone, camera, and a heart rate monitor. The idea behind it is, if you're in trouble, he can help you. He's also agreed to pay you an extra two hundred each month to wear it."

"Told you he loves me," I bragged. I felt so sure of myself in that moment, so on top of the world and like nothing could ever change that. The man I loved, who loved me as well, wanted to keep me safe so much he'd purchased some tech I knew to be expensive in order to ensure my well-being. That made me so freaking happy, I couldn't stop smiling.

Monroe snorted, but whatever he wanted to say to me couldn't touch my happiness in that moment. "If being stalked by someone makes you feel loved, then go for it, kid. Go on now, back to your brother, then off my planet."

I laughed as I walked past him. "It's not your planet. You don't own all of Wish. And it's not stalking. It's called love and wanting to keep me safe."

Monroe rolled his eyes, but I saw him smile a little as he locked the door up behind us.

Thank you for the bracelet, I sent off to Dragonfly while I was waiting for Corbin to return from his appointment.

It took a full half hour to get a reply back from him. *You're welcome. You wanted something personal about me, well here it is; I could kiss you for hours and never grow bored tasting you or hearing the little noises you make when my tongue is in your mouth and my hands are on your skin.*

I love you too.

Yours Always,

Dragonfly

That wasn't quite what I'd meant, but I wasn't going to argue with that as I turned bright red. I'd barely stopped blushing when Corbin entered his room, and when he asked about my bracelet, I told him Dragonfly had given it to Monroe to give to me. It was the truth. He just didn't need to know I'd been with Dragonfly. Though why I was keeping that from him, or why Monroe had asked me to, was beyond me. Still, I wasn't going to break Monroe's rules. I didn't want to risk him keeping Dragonfly from me or do anything to jeopardize Corbin's job at Asiq.

CHAPTER NINE

THE FIRST time I saw the bracelet light up was when I was running laps for class the next day. I was exhausted, barely able to breathe even though I was gasping hard to force air into my lungs and doubled over as my classmates passed me.

"Hurry up, Thierry! Get moving!" Mr. Allessan shouted.

I shook my head, straightened, and that's when I noticed the bracelet was glowing. I lifted my wrist and gave Dragonfly a scan of the area around me, just in case he thought I was being chased or something like that. After a few seconds, the bracelet went dark again, and I continued running until Mr. Allessan told us we could quit.

Once I'd showered and changed back into my uniform, I went back to my dorm, where I pulled out my holoscreen and wrote a quick note to Dragonfly.

> *Hey,*
> *Are some functions of the bracelet automatic? It lit up while I was running in class. I wish I knew who you were or could see you without your mask. I wouldn't tell anyone.*
> *Love you.*
> *Thierry*

I sighed happily and laid my head on the pillows. With so many people around me all the time, it was nice to have a break from the noise and constant pressure I felt to perform well. Everyone there wanted to be amazing. I was right there with them in that idea, but unlike most of my classmates, I knew that I'd been lucky to get in. They seemed to think it was their right to be there.

My holoscreen beeped, and I picked it up.

> *Thierry,*
>
> *Bracelet functions are automatic, but if you need me and it isn't activated, you can press down on the face for three seconds, which will signal me. When the bracelet lights up, I am given a message on my holoscreen, the video comes up, and I can choose to keep watching or shut down the connection. I saw that you were safe and let you go on with your day. I hope the rest of it is less strenuous. The bracelet is waterproof, so there is no need to take it off if you happen to go swimming. I can also hear you so if you do need help and need to get information to me, you may do so by speaking into the bracelet.*
>
> *I know how much you wish I could tell you who I am or give you some hint as to my identity. I cannot, and I hope, in time, you come to understand why or at least respect my decision to remain masked when I'm around you.*
>
> *Yours always,*
> *Dragonfly*

Dragonfly saying the bracelet was waterproof gave me a really good idea. But unfortunately I had classes the rest of the afternoon and couldn't do what I wanted to. I anxiously sat through my history lessons, chemistry, systems, and an impossibly long lecture on how to approach new species in order to effectively work with them on their home world.

It wasn't until after seven, when I'd finished a quick meal, that I was able to go into the showers to be alone while everyone else was doing their own thing. Not many people used the showers this early in the evening, but I was quiet as the hot water sprayed over me and I slowly began to stroke myself.

When the bracelet didn't light up right away, I pressed its face, waited for it to glow, and then let Dragonfly see my face. "Hey," I said, hoping he could understand me through the sound of the water coming down on top of me.

The bracelet stayed lit as I dropped my wrist to the side and held it there for him to see what I was doing as I played with myself. I didn't have time to stay under the spray of the water and give him a good show, but I hoped he liked it all the same.

I leaned against the tile wall as I thought about him: his mouth on me, him running his hand down my stomach to grip me as I was holding myself right now. I was afraid of getting caught, but I wasn't nervous about putting on a show for Dragonfly. I loved him, and I wanted to do this with him. I couldn't have him with me right then, but at least I could give him this.

I came hard as I fought not to cry out and managed to bang the back of my head against the tile, which hurt a lot. The bracelet stayed lit the whole time and only shut off after I brought my wrist up to my face and blew him a kiss. I then turned off the water and started drying myself off.

When I got back to my room and checked my holoscreen for messages, I was glad to see one waiting for me. Two, actually, but I swiped the one from Corbin aside to read after the one from Dragonfly. I was glad Monroe was fast in sending his messages through. Maybe, after so many, he had them automatically forwarded so he didn't have to sit there and send each one between us. I was also glad that he didn't read our messages. I didn't want

Monroe knowing what I did with Dragonfly, or how much I cared about him. That wasn't his business.

You have found a better use for the bracelet than I could have imagined. I look forward to seeing you again.

I grinned. I was already counting down the days until I had my next weekend off-world.

WHEN I didn't get the usual call three weeks later on the Friday before I was supposed to go to Wish, I called Monroe. "Hi, it's Thierry."

"What can I do for you, Thierry?" Monroe asked. He sounded a bit impatient, but at this point I figured that was just his personality.

"I'm off-world tomorrow...." I hinted.

"So you are. Is there anything else?"

I frowned and sat down on my bed. "Does he want to see me?" I wouldn't say his name, even though I was alone in my room. I didn't want anyone to possibly overhear my conversation with Monroe.

"Dragonfly will unfortunately not be in attendance this weekend, but you are still welcome to visit Asiq if you wish to see your brother. I'm sure the weeks apart are hard on you, as close as you two are."

I was instantly disappointed. "I'd like to come over tomorrow, then."

"Do you need me to schedule your trip?"

"Sure. Thanks." I was trying really hard not to be upset. I'd been looking forward to seeing Dragonfly, and he knew I only had one weekend off a month to be able to see him. He'd said he wanted to see me too. I didn't understand. "Are you sure he won't be there? Maybe he got confused on the dates."

Monroe sighed, and I figured it was the wrong thing to ask, but I couldn't take it back, and besides, I really did want to know.

"Thierry, I assure you he won't be here, but if you insist, I will call and remind him of the date. Perhaps he has other matters to attend to this weekend. The universe does not revolve around you and getting your five thousand credits."

It wasn't about the money for me, but of course Monroe wouldn't have understood that, and I was feeling so down I wasn't interested in explaining it to him right then. "Thanks for calling. I'll be there tomorrow. Same time."

"Very good. As always, the room next to your brother will be free for your use."

I nodded. "Thank you. Bye."

"Good-bye."

He hung up the com call, and I took out my earpiece and brought my knees up to my chest. It wasn't a total loss. I did miss Corbin. I only wished I'd gotten to see Dragonfly too, since it would be a whole month before I got to see him again otherwise.

WHEN I got to Asiq the next afternoon, I put my things in my room and went looking for my brother. I ended up finding him in the lounge with a bunch of bright lights and loud music everywhere. They were painting each other, and I laughed when I saw that someone had painted yellow dots all over Corbin's upper body to match the yellow around his face. He looked like he'd come down with some kind of yellow spotted disease.

"Ha-ha, Thierry. You're here now. It's your turn!" He grabbed my hand and pulled me forward.

"No! No, I'm good! I swear!" I batted his hand away, but the guys were already laughing and egging me on. The customers around us were all drunk, even though I could tell that my brother wasn't just by looking at him. He didn't drink often. Neither of us did since it messed with us too much, and even after one drink, he was pretty wasted.

"C'mon, little brother, everyone is doing it!" Corbin goaded me. In the end I took off my shirt and let someone I didn't know paint silvery hearts on my shoulder, since Corbin couldn't hear me arguing with him over the loud music.

Having paint on me wasn't so bad, but when someone went for the button of my pants, I got myself out of there in a hurry, despite the protests of the people calling to me and the customers laughing. The party went right on ahead as I slipped into the hallway. Corbin hadn't noticed my absence yet, but I figured once he did, he'd come looking for me.

It was Monroe who found me first, though.

"Hi," I said when I saw him coming up the hallway toward me.

"You aren't one of my men, and you aren't on display for everyone here to see, so don't dress like it," he scolded.

I quickly put my shirt back on. "Sorry. Just having a bit of fun," I mumbled as I came up to him.

He nodded and stood beside me in the narrow hallway. "Are you still interested in spending time with Dragonfly?" He kept his voice quiet, even though no one from the party could hear us.

I nodded instantly. "Of course. I love him."

Monroe pinched up his face, but after a second, he nodded. "Go to the room you normally share with him. He'll be with you in an hour. And get the paint off your shoulder. Silver doesn't go with your skin tone."

I flushed and started to move away. "But you said he wouldn't be here…."

"He decided to visit anyway. Do you want to see him or not, Thierry? I don't think I need to remind you I'm a very busy man with a business to run."

I laughed and shook my head. "You don't need to remind me. Thanks for letting me know. I'll be waiting for him."

"I'll let him know."

"Great. Thanks." I smiled and gave him a quick wave before I practically ran to the room with the red door. I was nervous, and eager, which made me distracted. I started running late while getting ready for him, but I managed it, even though my hair was wet and stuck up in short black spikes around my face as I put on the robe. On second thought, I decided to go without it.

I pressed the face of the bracelet in to get it to light up. "I can't wait to see you again. Thank you for coming to visit me," I said into it as soon as it was lit. The bracelet only stayed on for a few seconds before it went dark again. I went to stand next to the big four-poster bed and put my hand around one of the spiraled posts. I was ready for him, and I hoped he liked the surprise of me already being naked for him when he came in, though really, having a short robe on that barely covered my butt hardly kept me all that modest when I was around him.

He knocked and came in a few minutes later, and I smiled at him when he turned to see me standing there, waiting for him. There was no dinner this time, probably because it was such short notice, and so there was nothing to delay me having him again. He lifted me into his arms, and I crossed my ankles behind his back as I sank into his kiss.

He laid me down on the bed, and I sighed as he slipped his tongue into my mouth as he kissed me. "Fuck me, please...." I begged him. I normally didn't say anything like that to him and had never been so bold while talking to him, but by the way he groaned against my mouth, I figured I might have said the right thing.

I got a crazy, stupid idea in my head as he rubbed against me, teasing me with his length through his black pants. I put my hands on his shoulders, and he moved his mouth to my neck to kiss me by my ear.

I wanted to know who he was. I had to know. When I thought about him, I knew everything but his face and his voice. I didn't care that he was older than me, and I knew I wouldn't care if he had scars or something on his face. I loved him. I wanted to know who he was and what he looked like. Then we wouldn't have to pretend, and I could even have vidcalls with him when he wasn't busy. I slipped my fingertips under the edge of his mask. I could hear his voice. I could tell him I loved him, and he could say it back to me. In one quick motion, I yanked his mask over his head and got my first look at Dragonfly.

"You!" I gasped as I started fighting him and screaming at him.

"Thierry! Shut up!" Monroe nearly shouted at me, and when that didn't work, he clamped his hand down on my mouth, muffling my screams.

I was looking at him when I started to cry. I struggled to get up, but Monroe had my hands in his and pinned my wrists above my head. That meant I could scream if I wanted to. Too bad I no longer did.

"I can't believe you had sex with my brother when you seemed so into me. I hate you," I hissed as I tried to kick him off me. It was nearly impossible while I was pinned under him, and the worst part was I could feel him thick and hard against me, and I still wanted him even though I raged at him. I'd been in love with him for months. I'd wanted him for months. And he'd lied to me the whole time. "You're a deceitful, evil, mean person, and I hate you. You've been lying to me for months, screwing around with me, and you could have told me the truth at any time. Get off of me, or I'll start screaming again. And you had sex with my brother!"

I didn't understand why he looked hurt by my words, or why he thought it was still okay to put his mouth on my cheek. But when he tried to kiss me, I turned my head to the side. If he kept trying, I was planning to bite him and I'd make sure it hurt.

"Are you going to make me have sex with you, then? Is that your plan?" I felt sick asking him that question, but I didn't know what to think. All this time I'd been in love with Monroe. I'd wanted my brother's boss. I'd had sex with him. And so had Corbin.

I really was going to be sick.

Monroe sighed and got off me but blocked my way to the door. "No. I'd never do that. Especially not to you."

I sat up and moved to get my clothes on as quickly as I could. I'd been so stupid. I angrily wiped at my eyes and tried to go to the door once I was dressed, but he didn't move out of my way.

"Move," I demanded.

Monroe shook his head. "You can't go, Thierry. There aren't any shuttles to take you off-world for another three hours. Stay here tonight and think."

"No. I'm leaving. I'll go to another club and sleep there if I have to. I'm not staying anywhere near you." I practically spat the words, and I was glad when I saw him flinch away from me.

But when I tried to leave again, he put his hand firmly on my upper arm. I had tramped down on my nerves the second his mask was off, but it hurt to have him touch me because of how much I'd loved Dragonfly.

"If you walk out that door, I won't give you any more money."

I laughed at him and tried to break free of his hold, but he tightened his hand around my arm. "I'm not your personal whore, Monroe. Now let me go."

Monroe released me, and I tried going to the door again. "If you go, I'll cut your brother from the roster. He'll be broke and homeless."

That stopped me cold, and I turned to stare at him. He knew I'd do anything for my brother, including have sex with him just to keep Corbin there. Of course he did. He knew everything there was to know about me, and I felt torn apart and betrayed by him.

"You'd threaten me like that?" I asked, my words coming out harshly. It was getting harder not to cry in front of him by the second.

Monroe sighed loudly before he shook his head. He looked like he wanted to come toward me, but when I backed up, he stopped. "No. Not that."

I was nearly shaking by then. "What do you want?"

"Your silence. That's all. No one can ever know I paid you for sex or I won my own auction. I already have clients begging me for the next virgin, and it cannot get out I overbid them all intentionally just to have you. It would ruin my reputation as an upstanding businessman in this community. I'd lose everything. No one would ever trust me again, and trust is all you have on Wish."

I tried to care about what he was saying but couldn't bring myself to. As long as I didn't have to let him touch me again, I'd agree to anything he wanted. "Fine. Done." I nodded for emphasis.

"Then you may go. I'll book you passage on the same shuttle Corbin will be taking tomorrow morning. I won't bother you again, and Corbin will remain here for as long as he wants to, if you keep your promise."

"I will."

I left the room before he could say anything else and went straight to the one he'd given me my first night there, the one next to Corbin. I cried for at least an hour. And then I started throwing things. There was nothing to break in the room, so I tossed my clothes around and then felt incredibly stupid afterward.

I was still hurt but a lot of my anger had dissipated. I left the room and went back to the lounge, where music was still playing. I didn't see Corbin, but someone offered me a seat and I took it. Monroe stood next to the bar, overseeing his clients and his men, and when he looked at the guys dancing on the low stage in the center of the room, I knew what I wanted to do. He'd hurt me with his lies and playing with me, and if he loved me like he'd said, then my dancing with someone else should hurt him too. I wanted him to be angry like me, to be in pain like me, and I wanted him to be jealous. Mostly, though, I just wanted to hurt him in any way I still could. Everything I'd thought I'd known about Dragonfly, every kind word and soft touch had been a lie. It was just Monroe, a man that had sex with everyone in his brothel and who had used me.

So I stripped off my shirt, tossed it aside, and got up on stage amidst the catcalls of the clients and the smiling faces of the men who worked for the man I was in love with. I danced with the first guy who put his hands on me. He ground himself against my butt, and I didn't care because I was watching Monroe and waiting for him to do something, say something, to let me know it all hadn't just been some cosmic joke and a lie. I wanted to know he'd felt something for me too, that he'd actually cared. That he'd hurt me and was being hurt by what I was doing. But when the guy I was dancing with reached down to cup me, Monroe walked away. He didn't stop them from touching me, didn't say anything to me. If he'd cared I expected him to pull me off the stage, to explain things to me, to tell me that he'd actually loved me and it hadn't all been lies.

I knew then that I had to take it even further to get back at him, so when the guy asked me back to his room, I said yes and I made sure I laughed as loud as I could as we walked past Monroe's office, just in case he was in there and able to hear me.

"Fuck, you're beautiful," he told me once we were alone. I didn't say anything, just let him kiss me. He stripped off his pants and pushed me down on my knees. I sucked him and tried not to care that he wasn't Dragonfly, that I didn't know him and didn't love him. He pulled my hair when he wanted me back on my feet, and he put me on the bed.

I let him undo my pants. I let him stretch me, and then I let him screw me. It wasn't loving, it wasn't passionate. I pressed down on the bracelet, and when it lit up and I knew Monroe could see me, I faked enjoying it as he watched the guy kiss me from over my shoulder. I moaned like I wanted it. I begged him for more like I was enjoying it.

The bracelet went dark, and I dropped my head onto the blanket. He got off and used his hand to make me come.

"I thought Sythe were supposed to be something special," he told me as he was getting dressed. He sounded annoyed. I didn't actually care.

I shrugged and put my clothes back on. He looked disappointed, and I hated myself even more than before as I made my way back to my room. I went into the shower, turned the water on as hot as it would go, then cried as I scrubbed myself raw.

"HEY, YOU okay?" Corbin asked me as we left Asiq the next morning.

I nodded and forced a smile that felt as fake as my pleasure had been the night before. "Yeah. I'm good. Just tired."

Corbin smiled at me. "Some party, huh? I heard you had fun."

"Loads." He stopped talking about the party and focused on getting us back to the station, where the transport was waiting to take me back to the academy. I should have talked to Corbin more. I should have found something to say instead of wallowing in my own misery. But right then all I wanted to do was be alone with my pain and heartbreak.

CHAPTER TEN

WHEN I got back to class, I thought everything would be fine. It was good to be away from the distraction of Monroe, and it was easier not to think about him when I wasn't on Wish and around him constantly. But it hurt too, and even though I considered it every morning when I got up, I couldn't take off the bracelet he'd given me.

"Everything okay with you?" Quatar asked me a week later.

I looked up from the article I was studying on my holoscreen. "I'm fine. Why?"

Quatar shrugged. "Nothing. You're just really quiet."

"Everything's great. Absolutely perfect." It was a lie but whatever. He wasn't the first person to notice I was struggling. I wished it weren't so obvious I was miserable.

I'd stopped writing letters to Dragonfly, and by the time two weeks passed, I was feeling a bit better. That was, until my brother called me.

I put in my earpiece and remembered a second after answering the call that Corbin had had sex with Monroe. That thought left a really bad taste in my mouth as I tried not to think about my brother having sex with the man that I loved. Had loved. Maybe still loved. I really wasn't sure at this point.

"Hi," I said as I finally answered the call.

"Hey. I haven't heard from you lately. Something wrong? Classes okay? They're not being too hard on you, are they?"

I tried not to feel betrayed by him too. It wasn't his fault, and he didn't know. But it didn't hurt any less that he'd been naked with Dragonfly. My Dragonfly… er, Monroe. "I'm fine. Just busy."

"You sure?" He didn't sound convinced. I didn't blame him. I wasn't all that great sounding.

"Yep." I tried to be happy, to keep him from somehow knowing that I wasn't okay. But I was pretty sure it wasn't working. So I crashed. "Truth is…. Truth is, I like someone. A lot. And it's not gonna work."

"Why not?"

He made it sound so simple, like how dare someone not like me back. I should have never said anything. I hadn't expected him to have more questions, which was probably pretty stupid of me.

"He's not into guys." It was a complete and utter lie. But I couldn't exactly tell him the truth either. And I had to tell him something.

"Tough break. Sorry, Thierry."

I hated lying to my brother, especially since he sounded so sincere. "Thanks. I gotta go." I didn't really have to go of course, but I didn't want to accidentally spill the truth either. I was horrible at lying and absolutely disastrous at it when I was trying to lie to Corbin. At least he wasn't there with me to see me be untruthful to him. It wouldn't have been so easy to say those words to him if we'd been face to face.

"Talk to you later?" he asked, still not sounding convinced, but it was the best I could do when all I wanted to do was cry.

"Sure." I hung up before I could say anything else.

I was supposed to do endurance training in the form of running mindlessly around a track three times a week and hand-to-hand combat the other two days. But I'd skipped a lot of training since I didn't want the bracelet to light up and Monroe to see me again after last time, when I'd been having sex… or whatever that was. To me sex was good, it made me happy, and I'd always felt loved. I was glad I hadn't been looking at the guy—I hadn't even bothered to get his name—so I didn't have to remember him on top of me like I remembered Monroe. I guess I could have taken off the bracelet and just gotten on with my life, but I couldn't take it off. I'd tried, but I wasn't ready for that yet.

But that afternoon I was forced to go running when Mr. Allessan found me in the atrium. "Thierry, either run or get expelled," he told me as I stood looking out over the starships, wanting to be out in space already. Then maybe I could feel like I was able to actually get away from Monroe on some level.

"Is it serious that I've missed a few? I've been to all my other classes," I asked him, surprised that being expelled came down to attending all my gym sessions.

Mr. Allessan nodded. "It is. Now get down there. You've already missed your session for today, and everyone else is on their free hour right now, so I expect you to make full use of the empty track."

I sludged through it, even though it hurt to run that hard and I wanted to quit after only the second mile. The bracelet was lit up, but I ignored it, and it finally went dark again. By the time Mr. Allessan waved me over, I was sore and barely able to breathe as I clutched at my side.

"I expect you not to skip your sessions anymore," he told me as I practically limped over to him on wobbly legs. I'd never had to run that hard or that long before. It was like he was making me pay for missing nearly all my sessions that month.

I shook my head. "No...." I gasped for breath and spit into the dirt by my feet. "I won't."

"Good. Go shower."

Grateful for being dismissed, I walked slowly to the shower rooms. Once I was clean and redressed, I felt a little better, but as soon as I came out of the shower area and into the locker room, I found Mr. Allessan sitting there waiting for me.

"Did I forget something?" I asked him as I grabbed my bag out of my locker. I was ready to go and really felt like crashing into my bed for a little while. My whole body hurt from running that hard and my legs felt like they'd give out at any minute.

He got up from the bench he'd been sitting on and turned the holoscreen in his hands so that I could see it. I looked away from my ad when I had been on Asiq as quickly as I could and hoped I wasn't blushing.

"That's you, isn't it?"

"No." It was far easier to lie to him than to Corbin. I started walking past him, but he put his hand in the center of my chest and pushed me back against the lockers so hard I gasped and pain shot through my back. I dropped my bag as I stumbled. I stared up at him, scared of what he was going to do and knowing I couldn't stop him if he tried anything. I was too tired and sore from running, and he was at least twice my size. "Stop," I told him. "I'll scream."

He laughed at me. "Everyone is on their free time. That means there's no one around to hear you. Now, tell me the truth. Is this you? Are you a whore?"

I tried to get his hand off my chest, but he pressed it into me until I couldn't take a full breath. "I'm not," I said, my voice weak from the strain of getting the words out. I pushed at his chest, but he leaned into me, pinning me.

"I think it is. Show me what you can do, little whore, or I'll tell everyone here what you are and what you did to get into this school."

I gasped, staring up at him. I shook my head. "No."

"Thierry...," he warned. I knew he wasn't joking.

"No. I won't. Let me go."

His smile dimmed. "I'm not joking."

"And I'm not having sex with you," I spat at him.

He stepped back, releasing me, and I coughed as air rushed into my lungs. "You'll regret this."

"Fuck you," I growled, reaching down to grab my bag and run out of there. I was heading back to my dorm with my heart racing in my chest. I tried to hold back angry tears, but I was pretty sure they'd come anyway as soon as I stopped walking. I only hoped that I was alone when that happened.

I didn't get more than two feet into the dorms when I saw people staring at me. And then the laughing began, and someone held up their holoscreen and asked if that was me. It was my worst nightmare, having everyone find out what I'd done to get into their school. I spun on my heels and ran. I got as far as the shuttle bay before realizing I needed to get out of that system and not just off that planet.

I needed my brother, and I needed him right then and there, so I got on the shuttle and I got on the transport, and then I took the next shuttle to Wish. By the time I got to Asiq, I didn't think I had any more tears left to cry because I'd sobbed the whole way there.

As soon as I got through the back door, Monroe grabbed me by the sleeve of my jacket and pulled me into a spare bedroom, and I knew my luck had just gone from bad to crash-and-burn worse.

"You aren't welcome here anymore," Monroe barked, as if I'd ever want to be back there if it wasn't some kind of massive emergency. I pulled my sleeve over my palm and wiped at my eyes.

"I'm here to visit Corbin," I mumbled. I refused to look at him. I wanted to see my brother, and if I couldn't do that, then I sure as hell didn't want to be near Monroe. It was his fault all of this was happening anyway.

Monroe nodded. "You can visit him. But you can't stay more than a few hours and none of my men will even look at you, so don't think about having sex with any of them again. They know better than that now. I won't allow it."

"Fine. We done here?" I snapped, lifting my head to actually look at him for the first time.

He didn't say anything. Not at first anyway. Then he put his hand under my chin and forced me to tilt my head back so he could look at my face. "You've been crying. What happened?"

I ignored the heat of his fingertips on my skin or what it felt like to have him touching me again. I couldn't even begin to remember that. Those memories brought too much heartache with them. So I pulled away and wiped at my eyes again. Maybe if I rubbed at them enough, I wouldn't look like I'd been crying so much. Maybe Corbin would think I was having a reaction to something instead.

"You don't get to ask questions about my life anymore. You lied to me, used me, and betrayed me."

Monroe didn't try to touch me again. "I said I never lied to you. And I haven't."

I laughed, and it hurt. "What about having sex with my brother? I can't believe you'd do that to me. No, wait. I can. Because you never gave a damn about me more than sex, and everything else was just an act to get me back here each month."

"I'm done talking to you about that. Ask him about it yourself if it bothers you so much. Now tell me what happened to you." He sounded angry, and I glanced at him out of the corner of my eye before turning away again.

"One of my teachers had my ad. Wanted me to have sex with him, and I said no, so he sent the ad to everyone, I guess." I acted like it didn't matter, even though it was a huge deal to me. I didn't want him knowing how upset I was over it. I didn't want him knowing anything about me at all. He already knew too much as far as I was concerned.

Monroe tried to put his hand on my shoulder, probably to get me to look at him, but I shook off his hand. "What was his name?"

"What?"

"His name, Thierry. The man who tried to make you have sex with him. What. Was. His. Name?"

115

I was surprised to see him looking so upset when he clenched his hands into fists at his sides. "I never said he tried to make me...."

"I inferred it. Now, his name?"

I licked my lips nervously before answering him. "Mr. Allessan. I don't know his first name. He teaches my physical classes."

Monroe put an earpiece in his ear before touching a few buttons on the com on his wrist. "Mr. Allessan, Monroe here, owner of Asiq. I have a little problem. Are you busy?"

He sounded almost happy to talk to Mr. Allessan, and I wondered why that would be since he still looked really angry to me.

"Great," Monroe continued. "Well, you see it's about Thierry. I think you know who I'm talking about. Good, then we're on the same page." I could tell he was angry now by his voice. He sounded like he wanted to kill Mr. Allessan. I wasn't scared. I didn't even shiver. I kind of wanted Mr. Allessan to be ruined for humiliating me like he had, though I'd stop short at actually causing him any kind of physical harm. I wasn't that evil. "Thierry is not yours to touch, look at, talk to, or even think about except as it pertains to his education as a pilot, Mr. Allessan. And if you ever wish to step foot inside Asiq, or inside any other establishment on this fine planet, you will publicly apologize to Thierry for your mistake. You will tell everyone you were wrong and if, and only if, Thierry is satisfied with the changes in the school, I will allow you to come back as long as you agree to a probationary period for the rest of the time Thierry is at your academy. If anything else happens to him, including something indirectly happening as a result of your actions today, then you will be banned forever and blacklisted from this and every other pleasure planet in the universe. You forgot what kind of influence I have on the other people of this planet. I suggest you remember that the next time you choose to go after someone you think might be working for me. If you cross the line in any way with Thierry again, I will have you castrated before I have you killed. Do I make myself clear, Mr. Allessan?"

Monroe smiled, though it wasn't a happy one, and I wondered if Mr. Allessan was scared because if he wasn't, I was pretty sure he needed to be. "I'm glad you've come to see things my way. Pleasure doing business with you. Bye."

I stared blankly at him for a long moment before speaking. "I don't know why you did that for me. You didn't have to."

Monroe sighed, and it sounded like he was getting fed up with me. The feeling was pretty mutual since I still hadn't forgiven him, even after weeks spent apart. "Again, I never lied to you. I hid my identity from you, I refused to answer direct questions about who I was, but I never actually lied to you. Including when I told you I loved you. I did then and I still do now."

I licked my lips and had to look away. The room was suddenly too small, and I had too many thoughts in my head to settle on just one, but somehow, after a few long moments of silence between us, I managed it.

"Why did you have sex with Corbin if you love me so much?" I asked. It was the only answer that really mattered to me.

Monroe shook his head and crossed his arms as he stared me down. "I told you to ask your brother about that."

I was too stubborn for that. "I'm asking you."

He groaned and unfolded his arms. He rubbed his hands together, and in a flash I remembered what it was like to have his hands on me, to feel him touching me, to feel loved with just an embrace. I was bright red and hoped I didn't reveal myself and what I was feeling.

"Fine, if you wish to know the truth—"

"I do."

When I didn't turn to him, he came over to stand against the wall with me, crowding me. I could have moved back. I could have gone across the room to be away from him. But I couldn't get my feet to work.

"I never had sex with your brother," Monroe told me. His voice was soft, and he sounded so sincere I almost thought he was being honest.

"But he—" I frowned and shook my head. Corbin had told me he'd been with Monroe. There was no reason for him to lie.

"He needed a part on his shuttle fixed and asked for a loan. I told him I didn't do loans, but I would give him the money if he agreed to tell you that one lie. He didn't know why, and he never asked me about it."

I glanced at him. "But why lie to me? Why make him tell me that?"

Monroe gave me a soft smile that looked just this side of sad, which I didn't understand. He had no reason to be upset since he was the one who had hurt me with his deception, not the other way around.

"Because you told me you loved me. You didn't know anything about me except I was willing to pay you for sex and had an interest in your well-being, yet you believed you loved me. I had to kill the delusion of a silly little child before you truly fell in love with me."

I scowled up at him. "I do. I mean, I did." I'd always loved him.

Monroe shook his head. He put a hand gently on my shoulder, and I didn't pull away. "I own a brothel. I'm around men who wish to make money by selling their bodies nearly every minute of the day. I'm asked at least a few times a week to have sex with them, either for large amounts of money, favoritism, or because they simply want to bed their boss. And before you came along, I even took some of them up on it. I knew that eventually you would know who I was, simply because a hidden truth is hard to keep up forever when your brother works here and is one of my best, and so I needed you to not want me once you found out. And it worked. You didn't. I haven't received a note from you in weeks. And once you knew who I was, you even took another man to your bed, one of my own employees in fact."

I didn't need the reminder, and I didn't like thinking about that night. "I know. I was there."

He moved his hand to my chest, and I let him touch me, though I still couldn't put my hands on him. I wasn't ready to open myself up to him either. I knew it would hurt too much to allow myself to feel that kind of pleasure with him again.

"You didn't look like you were enjoying it from what I could see."

"It was a mistake." I was whispering because that wasn't something I was proud of. Not any of it. I'd only been with two people so far in my life; one I had loved and honestly still did, though it was much easier to pretend otherwise when he wasn't touching me, and the other man I didn't even know the name of and had been using to punish Monroe. That seemed to have backfired on me. That whole night had been pretty horrible overall and I wished I could take it all back. I was glad that I knew who Monroe was, but I wanted to go back to where it was just Dragonfly I was with, and Dragonfly who I loved.

Monroe nodded. When he moved his hand up to cup my cheek, I leaned into his touch. It was nice to be touched again, to have his hand on me. I wouldn't let him do whatever he wanted to me, but I wouldn't have said no if he kept touching me, either.

"So often things done or said in the heat of an argument are. You were feeling hurt and betrayed. No one would blame you for what you did, and you should let go of the guilt you feel."

I closed my eyes and took a deep breath. He knew how I'd felt, but that didn't do anything to erase what I'd done. "I let a stranger have sex with me."

He chuckled, and I quickly opened my eyes to stare up at him as I wondered what he could possibly find funny in that moment. "Are you referring to our multiple times or the one time you actually saw your lover's face?"

"With you it was different." He had to know that. If he didn't I was sure he was stupid.

Monroe dropped his hand. I wish he hadn't, but I wasn't about to tell him to keep touching me. "No, it really wasn't."

I stepped toward him, closing a little of the distance between us. "It felt like it."

"Then you have a lot of growing up to do. Unfortunately I don't have the time to teach you at the moment, as I am a very busy man who has a business to run and this little chat has taken up enough of my time. You are no longer banished from these premises, but I trust you won't be staying here past the time of the first shuttle off-world tomorrow morning. Correct?"

I laughed at his reminder that he was a busy man, as always. I caught him smiling at me too, and it felt good not to be quite so angry at him for once. "Yes. I'll be gone soon enough."

He shook his head, though. "You don't have to sound so bitter about it. Until just now it seemed as if you never wanted to see me again. And really, who could blame you, now that you know the truth? I'm far older than you. Possibly even in the category of a lecherous old man."

I shrugged. I knew he was older, maybe even twice my age. But I couldn't really bring myself to care. "I'm not a stupid child either, you know, I did care about you. And I know you cared about me too." At least I hoped he did. I didn't want to be proven wrong again.

Monroe smirked and reached over to touch me, just for a moment, on my cheek, before he pulled away again. "And therein lies the problem. You aren't a child, but you aren't so sure of yourself that you could handle a relationship with me as I really am either. Dragonfly was a nice person to be for a while—thank you for that. I enjoyed what we had, but that's not who I am, not every day. And eventually the facade would have cracked, and you would have seen me as I really am. It's better it ended so quickly. For both of us."

I didn't believe him. I could have had my Dragonfly for years, but I knew I was to blame for ending it between us by taking off his mask. "Did you ever love me?" I was afraid to ask, but I had to know.

"You know the answer to that," he said before leaving the room.

I went out too, but I didn't go after him. I saw Corbin down the hall and went to him.

"Hey," I said, surprising him as I came up to his shoulder.

"Thierry? What are you doing here?" He threw his arms around me, even though he looked pretty shocked I was there.

I forced a big smile on my face as I hugged him back. "I snuck out for a bit. I wanted to see you."

Corbin shook his head as he let me go. "You shouldn't do that. What if they kick you out? You did so much to get into the academy, too much to risk just to come see me."

I knew he was right, and honestly I hadn't even thought about that in my rush to just get out of there. But I still tried not to show my worry as I came up with yet another lie for him. "It's okay. I got permission. It was a slow day, and I'm ahead in my classes, so they said it was fine for me to take a day off. I have to go back tomorrow morning. First thing."

It was only a slight lie since I was ahead in my classes and I would be leaving right away in the morning.

Corbin smiled at me and threw an arm over my shoulders. "Great. It's awesome that you're here to visit."

He took me into the lounge, where he made himself a drink and I dove into the chocolates. I saw the guy I'd had sex with, but he ignored me and I pretended not to notice him. For the rest of the night, I hung out with my brother whenever he wasn't with a client and tried not to think about Monroe.

When it was late and I was too exhausted to keep going, Monroe gave me my usual room. Corbin was with a client next door, and I hesitated at the entrance to the room beside Monroe.

"Thanks for what you did today. Talking to Mr. Allessan and letting me hide out here for a while," I told him.

Monroe nodded. "You're welcome. If anything isn't up to your standards at the academy, don't hesitate to call me. I'll take care of it. Someone in my position has a certain amount of pull in a lot more circles than you'd believe."

I didn't have to ask what that meant. He probably saw a fair number of important people come through Asiq each day. "Thanks

121

again." I hesitated. A big part of me wanted to kiss him. I didn't want him, wouldn't be having sex with him again, but part of me did want to kiss him. I put my hand on the doorknob as I decided what to do.

"Good night, Thierry. Have a better day tomorrow," Monroe told me before he made the decision for me by walking away and leaving me alone with my thoughts.

CHAPTER ELEVEN

THE NEXT evening I sat down to write my first note to someone other than my brother in nearly a month.

> *Monroe,*
> *I got my public apology this morning from Mr. Allessan. It was actually kind of funny, because he is being put on probation for his moral misconduct by visiting your site. I watched the faces of the other people in the room when they were talking about that, and I think you have a lot of customers who are teachers and administrators here. None of them looked all that thrilled with the decision by the dean.*
> *I was forgiven for leaving yesterday too. But I do have an inbox full of assignments I needed to make up. So it seems like you cleared up everything with your call. Wish I had that kind of pull sometimes. Maybe someday.*
> *Thierry*

It was good to write to him again, because I'd missed it. I looked down at my wrist, at the bracelet I hadn't taken off, and realized after weeks of having it on, I wasn't going to take it off anytime soon. Monroe wasn't Dragonfly to me, and I couldn't pretend, but I was slowly starting to get over hating him because I did understand, and someday I'd tell Corbin everything that had happened, but I didn't know how he'd feel about it either. I mean, Monroe was his boss, and he was a lot older than me. But I'd loved him as Dragonfly and someday I could maybe love him as he really was too.

The next day I hadn't heard back from Monroe yet, but after I started a note to Corbin, I couldn't get the words down because I was spending so much time thinking about Monroe. I ended up writing to him first. I sat on my bed with my head bent over the holoscreen in my lap and the stylus in my right hand while I wrote.

> *Monroe,*
> *We used the flight simulator today, and I managed to go to the docking station for the first time without hitting anything on the way back in. I'm sort of known in the academy as the guy that killed the highest number of digital people in one attempt at docking. It's not a good thing to be thought of like that. I'm looking forward to being a copilot in a few years, but it'll be a long time before anyone lets me have my own ship. Still, if I continue doing well, I'll get there eventually. I know it. And I saw an ad for a cruise line that's hiring. Getting on with something like that at some point would be good.*
> *Thierry*

Once I was done with my letter to Monroe, I knew I needed to write to Corbin too, or else he'd start getting worried.

Hey, I started my letter to him.

> *Miss you. Think this is the longest we've ever had to stretch being apart. It's weird not being at home, but I've got a few more years of it and have barely*

124

*started. I'm jealous of all the people who live on the
planet. There is a lot to see and do here on the
weekends when I can't go off-world, but my favorite
times are when I get to come to Wish and see you and
hang out there.*
Thierry

With my letters done for the day, I headed out of the dorms and down to the atrium, which had quickly become my favorite place in the academy. I looked down at the ships with the big windows letting in a lot of sunlight all around me.

My holoscreen beeped, and I pulled it out of my bag, expecting a message from Corbin but instead seeing one from Monroe. I went down to the cafeteria to grab a little dinner while I read his message.

I got fruit, milk, and a piece of bread with a soft cheese spread over it before finding a seat at the far edge of the cafeteria where I could still be in the sun while I read the message.

Thierry,
*Whatever you end up doing with your life, I'm
sure you'll do well in it. If anything changes for you at
school, let me know immediately.*
Monroe

My note back to him was a simple *Thank you*. I couldn't think of anything else to say to him. I still felt betrayed and lied to, but without the hate fueling me along in every conversation I had with Monroe and tainting each little thought of him, it was hard to know what to say. I loved him, but I realized I didn't know him. I felt like the fool I knew I was, but at the same time, it was hard not to pick up my holoscreen again and tell him how much I loved him.

All I knew for sure, and the only thing I was absolutely certain of, was that I wasn't going back to Wish anytime soon. But that meant not seeing my brother either, which sucked. I didn't get a call from either Monroe or Corbin when it was my chance to go off-world, but I did get a letter from Corbin on Sunday night when he got back home.

Hey. Wish you could have come to see me.
Missed you. I know you're busy, though. Another
month maybe?

He probably didn't mean to make me feel guilty, but that's how I felt after reading his note. I knew I had to talk to him, even if it meant disobeying Monroe. It was too late to go off-world, since everyone had to be back at the academy within two hours, so I found a quiet space in the library and sat down at a table to call him.

"Hi," I said as soon as I heard him pick up the call.

"Hey. You get my note?"

I glanced around the room to make sure I was alone. "I did. You have time to talk?" There were a few people hanging out, but none of them were close enough to hear my conversation. I kept my voice low just in case.

"Sure. What's up?"

I took a deep breath and tried to figure out where to begin. "First things first, what I want to tell you can't be repeated. Not to anyone. And you can't go beat up this person at all. You have to promise me that. It's important, so you absolutely have to promise."

"Sure. Whatever you want."

I shook my head. "You have to promise," I repeated and hoped he understood.

Corbin sighed loudly. "Yes, Thierry, I promise, okay? Now tell me what's going on. Did you cheat on a test or something?"

"What? No." I was actually kind of insulted he'd even think that. "I fell in love with someone. But I can't be with him. At least, I don't think I can. I'm so angry at him, but then again, I'm not, and it's all such a mess."

"Is this the guy who isn't gay? Because I can tell you that falling for a straight guy is one of the universe's worst and cruelest jokes. It's best to let him go and—"

"I lied about that."

Corbin didn't say anything for a few seconds. "Why?"

I didn't know how to tell him everything he needed to know, or how to even make it all make any kind of sense. I wasn't good at being concise, especially when my emotions got in the way of what I was trying to say. So I just hauled off and said it.

"I'm in love with Monroe, and he was Dragonfly, and it was great while he was like that, but then I pulled off his mask, and then I really hated him. And sometimes I think I still do. But then there was this teacher, and he tried to get me to have sex with him, and I told Monroe and then Monroe fixed everything, and now I don't know if I really hate him. I still love him, I still miss him. And sometimes I'm still really angry at him. And you can't say anything because he made me promise not to tell you, and he said that if I ever told anyone, you'd lose your job and you'd be homeless. And when I was really mad at him, I was hurt and had sex with someone, and I don't even know his name. And—"

"Okay, whoa. Slow way down and take a breath."

I did, and it helped to calm my racing thoughts. I wiped at my eyes because my vision was suddenly blurry. I hadn't realized I was crying. I took another really deep breath while I waited for him to say something, anything, just as long as he wasn't mad at me for lying to him or keeping secrets from him. Or for falling in love with his boss, either.

"When did you realize you loved him?"

I had to think back on that part. "A few months ago, I think. Maybe even a little longer than that."

"And you didn't say anything to me?"

I cringed. I knew that voice. He was angry, and I didn't blame him one bit for feeling that way. "I was in love with someone who wore a mask," I reminded him in a hushed whisper.

"And someone tried to force you to have sex with them? And you didn't tell me that, either?"

"Well...."

"And then you had sex with someone else and didn't even get his name?"

I lowered my forehead to the desk and sighed loudly. "I know it sounds bad."

"It sounds horrible, is what it sounds. What in the universe, Thierry? You didn't tell me anything about any of that. I thought school was going well, and you visited once a month to see me and everything was great. Wait, when you came here to see me, were you actually seeing him?"

"I was seeing you both," I told him defensively. "You have a regular Saturday night client that takes a few hours. I'd wait for you to go, and then I'd see him. We were always done by the time you were."

"And then he threatened you. Seriously, is there any point at which I'm not supposed to go kill him?"

"Please don't," I said weakly.

"Tell me why not, and maybe I won't. Give me one good reason."

I only had one really good one, and I'd already said it. "Because I love him."

"No. You're twenty, and he's in his forties. Wrong, try again."

I lifted my head from the table and glared at the com on my wrist. I couldn't glare at my brother, and that was the closest I could get to him. "So? I still love him. You can't decide that."

"And you can't decide to have a relationship with someone who is more than double your age and runs a brothel." I heard him throw something and hoped it wasn't anything important to him. Or anything of mine, for that matter. "And whom I had sex with."

I knew he was lying, not just because I believed Monroe, but because he'd waited too long to bring that up. "No, you didn't. He told me about the part you needed for your shuttle."

"Well, damn. I was hoping that would make you angry."

A smile cracked through my frown. "It did. When I pulled off his mask and finished being angry at him for hiding his identity from me, I got really angry at him for having sex with you. I felt hurt and betrayed, and even though you didn't know I loved him or that Monroe was Dragonfly for a little while there, I didn't like you much, either."

It felt good to be telling him all of this, to get the truth out there between us. We'd never had secrets from each other after our parents died. There were times when he didn't tell me how very sick he was while he worked in the mines, or there were times when he lied about not being hungry so I could have a full meal, but we'd never full-out lied to each other. Not until I'd met Dragonfly.

"You know if I'd known, I never would have said that, right? And if you're ever in love with someone in the future, I'd never have sex with them, even if they tried to be my client, right? I need you to know that."

"Yeah. I know."

"Good. Thank you. So, what can I do to help you get over Monroe?"

I shook my head because, while I knew he was trying to help, he wasn't really doing a good job of it. "I don't want to be over him."

"You can't be with someone more than double your age. You just can't."

"And I'm not," I replied, bristling as my anger rose. "We aren't together. At all." I took a deep breath and relaxed my tightly gripped fists on the table until my palms were flat on the cold, shiny steel beneath me. "And so what if I was? I wouldn't stop you from being with someone in their sixties. I didn't choose to be in love with him, it just happened."

Corbin groaned, and I really hoped he would come to his senses and not try to argue with me about this. "Okay, age aside, he owns a brothel. Let's call it like it is, Thierry. He has sex with guys who get paid to have sex."

"If you were ever serious with someone outside of Asiq, they'd be having sex with a guy who gets paid to have sex with other guys," I said right back to him.

"True. That's fair."

"And I'm not with him. I don't forgive him for lying to me."

"But you still love him?" Corbin's voice had gone softer, like he was losing some of his anger and maybe even trying to understand what I was feeling, maybe, just a little. I didn't think Corbin would be that okay with me being in love with Monroe anytime soon. I wasn't that naive.

I propped my chin up on my fist. "Yeah. And I miss him sometimes."

Corbin sighed, and I knew I might not have won, exactly, but I was closer to it than I had been. "And the guy that tried to force you? Is that taken care of? Is he dead? Because if he's not, I'd like him to be."

Smiling, I looked around the now empty room, and I was glad that I'd managed to keep my voice down for our whole conversation. "It's done, but he's not dead. Monroe threatened him with banishment from Wish if he tried anything like that with me again."

"He's a client? What's his name?"

"Mr. Allessan." I didn't hesitate in telling him because if he was one of Corbin's regulars, I didn't want him with my brother. Not only was it was creepy for my brother to have sex with one of my teachers, but also because I liked to think of all of Corbin's people being nice to and caring about him. Like the little old lady Monroe had told me about, or how Monroe had been with me when he was Dragonfly and I was just a naive little boy in love with a man in a mask.

"Okay. He's not one of mine, but if I see the name on the guest list, I'll make sure to steer clear. I'll let the others know too. Monroe may welcome him back on Wish, someday, but I have friends here and even though we can't refuse to be with someone, we can do other things to get out of it if the reasons are personal. And being a guy that tried to force my brother to have sex with him is a pretty big reason to stay away from him. But are you sure you're okay? Lots of bombshells here. Almost like a supernova or something massive like that."

I smiled. That's what it had felt like for me too. "I'm okay. I don't know when I'll be able to come back to Wish to see you, though."

"Don't worry about it. Now that I know, I completely understand. And I'm glad I have the next two weeks off. That way I can figure out how to pretend I don't know about everything when I'm around Monroe next."

"Thank you."

"Thanks for telling me. Don't lie to me or hide things from me again, though. That's not okay at all. I'm mad at you for that. Seriously."

I smiled. "Okay. I promise."

"Good. Do you need to get back to stuff?"

I did have some studying to do. "We learn about the Mian system tomorrow. I have a lot of reading to do beforehand."

Corbin laughed. "I'm sure you do as that system has three natural life planets in it and two more terraformed to go with them."

Groaning, I shook my head. "I didn't even know that. Want to come take the class for me and then I can sleep in?"

"Not a chance. Night, Thierry."

"Night." I hung up and took the earpiece out of my ear. Talking to him had made me feel better about everything, and I wished I'd done it sooner.

CHAPTER TWELVE

IT WAS three more months before I got up the nerve to call Monroe again on the Friday night before I was allowed to go off-world. Most of my classmates were going to some party on the planet's third moon. It was supposed to be a big deal, and I'd been invited, for once, which was great and meant that maybe I was making some actual friends there. Finally. But I hoped I could convince Monroe to let me make other plans.

"Hello?" he answered.

"Hi. It's—"

"I know who you are, Thierry. What can I do for you?"

He sounded happy, almost. And definitely warm. It took me a moment to remember why I'd called when all I wanted to do was climb onto his lap and kiss him when he sounded like that.

"My weekend off-world is tomorrow. I was wondering if I could come to Wish."

"You're no longer banished. I thought that had been made clear to you the last time you were here. If that's the reason you've been staying away, then I'm sorry."

I shook my head and gripped the edge of the bed tighter. "It's not. I mean, I knew I could go there. But I was hoping to see you tomorrow if I did."

"Oh." He sounded surprised, and I frowned, getting worried.

132

"Are you busy?" I shook my head because, when it came to him, that was a stupid question. "Never mind. You're always busy."

"Yes, I am typically occupied."

I licked my lips and tried not to voice my next thought, but it came out anyway. "Are you with someone now, then? Is that why I can't see you?"

"I never said you couldn't."

I relaxed my fingers enough to drum them on the side of the bed. "True. You didn't. But are you, though?"

"Seeing someone?"

My breath caught in my throat. He couldn't. We weren't together, but still, he just couldn't. I loved him too much. "Yes."

"No, Thierry. I'm not with anyone. Are you?"

"No." I wanted to tell him I loved him, and I didn't even look at the other guys here, but I was still so confused sometimes. But then other times, everything seemed to be so perfectly clear to me and I knew that I loved him. Despite everything else, of course I did, and I was stupid for not seeing that.

"Can you make your usual early morning flight?" Monroe softly asked, pulling me from my tangled thoughts.

"If you arrange it, I'll be there."

"Good. You said you wanted to spend time with me. Would you like that to include dinner? Just the two of us, no mask."

"Yes." I smiled, even though I was nervous to see him again.

"Be ready in the morning then."

"I will. Thank you."

"See you tomorrow."

I hung up, knowing I was in for a long, anxious night as I waited for time to go by before I could be on Wish again.

CORBIN HUGGED me as soon as I came through the front doors of Asiq the next afternoon. I'd been worried about what he'd say or do as it was the first time I'd seen him since telling him I was in love

133

with Monroe, but he hugged me, grabbed the bag out of my hand, then slung his arm around my shoulders like nothing had happened as we walked from the lounge where he'd been hanging out and back to the rooms.

That was until we got to my room and the door was closed behind us. "You here to see just me or Monroe too?" he asked me. I took my bag back from him and tossed it on the bed before I sat down.

He joined me, and I turned to look at him. "Both of you. Is that…. Are you okay with that?"

He pursed his lips and stared across the room. "If I tell you no, will you end things with him right now and tell him you never want to see him again?"

I didn't want to hurt him, but I didn't see anything wrong with what I was doing with Monroe either. We were just two people who talked sometimes and had loved each other weeks ago. In some ways—no, actually in a lot of ways—I still loved him, but I was pretty certain he didn't love me back. Not anymore.

"I can't do that, Corbin. Please don't ask me to."

He frowned, then sighed, and finally flopped backward on the bed to stare up at the ceiling. I sat silently next to him, waiting for him to do something, which I was pretty sure would be him yelling at me for how stupid I was being to think I was in love with someone so much older than myself. And maybe he was right. But I didn't think I was, and I didn't see anything wrong with it. I hardly knew Monroe, but I loved him, as backward and strange as that was.

"Don't let him hurt you. Please?" Corbin finally said as he turned to look at me. "Don't be reckless, don't be stupid for him. Don't fall in love with the wrong person because you think you need to or you owe him something for paying for your school. You have the credits in full. You don't owe him a damn thing. Don't let him make you think otherwise."

I looked at him for a long moment. "You sound like you're speaking from experience," I finally joked, laughing off the seriousness of his words and the pain in his eyes.

I wanted him to laugh it off too, tell me he was just playing, do anything but slowly nod in my direction. "I was younger than you and our parents were still alive, so that should tell you how long ago it was, but I fell in love with the wrong person. I thought he was the right one, and at one point I thought we would be in love together, and he would marry me and everything would be perfect."

"But it wasn't?"

Corbin shook his head. "No, it wasn't."

I'd had no idea and still couldn't picture who he was talking about. There'd been no one important in his life as far as I could tell. It was just him and me and our parents, until it was just us.

"What happened?"

Corbin gave me a sad smile. "He wouldn't disgrace his family by being with me."

"Because you're Sythe?" I asked, not understanding what he was saying.

Corbin laughed and shook his head. "No, silly, because I'm gay. And being with me made him gay, or at least bi. And he couldn't do that."

I leaned forward and propped my elbows up on my knees. "So what happened?"

"He went on with his life, I went on with mine. It's not that big of a deal, but it was a hard life lesson to handle. He was my first love, my first everything, really."

"You never told me. Or Mom or Dad, either. I didn't know."

Corbin shrugged. "What was I supposed to say? It was done and over with. Sometimes these things don't work out. I'm only telling you now because I want you to think first, before you lose yourself in a relationship that might not happen."

"It will—"

"Don't do that, Thierry. Don't be stupid and stubborn at the same time. You're twenty. He's much, much older than you. Don't force a relationship that isn't meant to exist. I'm not saying it's not, I'm just saying don't get hurt because you need something to be there that isn't. Relationships take work from both sides of the table, and you wanting something, no matter how much, won't automatically make it happen."

I knew what he was saying, and I appreciated it. "I'll try." I couldn't promise him anything more than that.

"Thank you."

He gave me a smile, a big one this time. "So tell me all about that time you crashed the simulated transport ship into the dock and killed all those digital people. You didn't really screw up that badly, did you?"

I groaned and fell back on the bed beside him. "I did. You should have seen the faces of the people around me, including the teacher's. I was so sure they were going to throw me out right then and there."

He laughed, and I smiled, because this was the brother I knew, the one who could tease me and delight in my embarrassment, not the sad man who still looked like he was in pain from someone rejecting him years and years ago.

ABOUT AN hour later, Corbin went to his usual Saturday night client, and I sat up in bed to call Monroe and see where he wanted to have dinner.

"Hello?" he answered my call.

"Hey. It's Thierry. I'm on Wish, and I was wondering where you wanted me to go for our dinner."

He chuckled, and I wondered what was so funny. "You're in Asiq. You've been here for the past few hours."

I frowned. "How'd you know that?" I hadn't seen him when I'd come in so unless someone told him I was there for some reason....

"I have cameras everywhere. Turn to your left. You see the little black dot by the window?" I turned and looked, but it was only about the size of my thumbnail and not nearly big enough for a camera. "I can see the entire room from that camera. Wave, Thierry."

I flipped him off instead. "Where do you want to have dinner?"

"The usual room is fine. I chose it originally for its privacy, after all. Will you be ready in an hour?" he asked.

"I'm ready now." I wasn't getting bathed and changed for him like I had all the times before. It wasn't that kind of date, and I wasn't getting paid for my time this trip, though he had covered my transport off-world as usual.

He chuckled again, and the sound of his happiness made me shiver. I turned away from the camera so he couldn't see my reaction to him or his voice. "I'm not. I'll see you there in an hour. Wear your jacket. I haven't had a good chance to see you in your uniform yet." I was glad I'd turned away so he couldn't see me blushing.

"Sure. Bye."

I hung up quickly, then lay back on the bed. I knew he could see me, but I was pretty sure he couldn't hear me since he hadn't burst down the door to stop Corbin and me from talking about him. I was anxious and excited, and normally that meant I would go for a run to work the energy out of myself. Just because I'd been skipping classes didn't mean I didn't enjoy running. I'd been outside nearly every chance I got, or at least sitting in the sun. Our apartment on the station didn't get much sunlight and the crowded steel catwalks weren't a good place to exercise.

But I didn't know my way around Wish, and I didn't want to get lost, so I was stuck there for the next hour with too much energy coursing through me and not enough room to use it up. I ran my hands through my hair, decided to suck it up, and pulled out my holoscreen to hopefully lose myself in some studying while I waited for the hour to be up.

He called me about five minutes later while I was reading about jump gate protocol. "Hello?" I answered, putting the earpiece in my ear.

"What are you reading?" No hello, just a question, as if we were back to being friends. I smiled.

"A chapter on jump drives and jump gates. Fascinating stuff." I wasn't being sarcastic. I really did love to learn about them, and I was looking forward to a time when I could go through them on my own. They were incredibly safe and nearly automatic for pilots, but I wanted to be the one to position the ship and press the throttle forward to make it go through the gate and into that controlled wormhole. I bet it was a rush.

"I'm sure it is. You look like you're enjoying yourself."

It sounded like he was smiling, and I imagined he was. "Aren't you supposed to be busy?" I teased him as I crossed my ankles over my butt.

He chuckled. "I am. Someone is getting written up tonight after I have dinner with you."

I looked at the camera and asked, "Corbin?"

"No, your brother is one of my best. This particular troublemaker has been digging himself a shallow grave for a while now."

I went back to looking at the pictures of my holoscreen as soon as he said Corbin was off the hook. I wasn't studying anymore, but I wanted to focus on something other than looking at the camera.

"What do you think of a man who is in this line of work?" I asked. I was curious, though I realized how that might be interpreted as a loaded question.

"Why, thinking about making a career out of it?"

I laughed and shook my head. I put my holoscreen aside, not wanting to look like I was trying to study while I talked to him. As I looked up into the camera, it was like we were having a real conversation instead of talking through the com on my wrist.

"No, definitely not. So…?"

"What do I think of the men I employ?"

I nodded. "Yes."

"Honestly, I think a lot of them have issues that should not be dealt with by having sex with strangers. I think they sometimes get the wrong idea of things, or they become emotionally invested in their clients, like the one I have to write up. But those kinds of men typically don't last long here. There's no room for them in an establishment like mine, but there are plenty of true, low-class brothels with hardly any standards that will take someone with problems that make them unfit to work for me."

I had figured at least some of that out from what I'd already been told by both Corbin and Monroe. "What about the guys who like it? Like Corbin?"

"They are the jewels of this industry. A true aspasian, one that gets off helping others, that is what I need more of. I dread the day your brother falls in love and no longer wants to work for me."

"He said he wouldn't leave, even if he did find someone. I asked him once," I told him. I doubted it was all that big a secret, as Monroe seemed to know Corbin pretty well from what I could tell.

"He may not want to, but not many men would let someone they're seeing be with strange men. It takes someone very open-minded to accept that sort of relationship, and very few people are. I have yet to meet one, though I've had to ban plenty of men who come to confront their boyfriends while they're working here. I have no tolerance for that, and relationships should never spill over into work here. That's just bad business."

That made sense. I knew I wouldn't be okay with knowing the person I loved was with other people too. "Were you ever an aspasian?"

"No. I bought the original building for Asiq from someone looking to sell. His whores—and I use that term rarely, but it absolutely applied to the people he employed—were all fired less than a week later, and I slowly built up my aspasians, gathered my clients, and filled a vital need on Wish for an experience, more than a quick round of sex. I don't suppose I'm going to get any more work done, so if you're ready now, we can start toward the room."

"I am." I got off the bed, gave him a little wave through the camera, and then hung up. He was waiting for me when I got there and quickly ushered me inside. He was probably worried someone would see us.

Being in the room with him, even though things were completely different between us, was still a bit strange. "It's a little surreal," I said as I went to the dish of chocolates I used to snack on before Dragonfly arrived. I didn't take one now, only touched the rim of the bowl before moving away again.

"Because you aren't naked?"

He was teasing me, and I gave him a little smile. "A little. And because you aren't wearing your mask. I like you better without it."

Monroe nodded and sat down at the little table where a plate of cheese, some smoked meats, and a few pieces of fruit were already waiting for us, along with a bottle of wine and two glasses. He poured a glass for me while I sat down.

"How are classes?" he asked me as we started eating.

I shrugged. "Good, I guess. I mean, I have a lot of tests right now and some of the practical ones are hard. I can't believe I'm being tested in the physical stuff too. There's points for hand-to-hand combat and running, where I'll lose points if I'm not as fast as everyone else. It's strange."

"And Mr. Allessan? Is he being good to you?" Monroe continued after he'd taken a sip of wine.

I took a break from the meats to drink too. "He's leaving me alone, so I guess that's the same thing. Everyone accepted his apology and bought that he made a mistake. He's still on probation at school." That made me smile. I ate some smoked fish.

Monroe laughed. "It'll be a long time before he gets off my shit list. Even if I didn't care about you, and you were just another person in my employ, I still would have gone off on him for what he did and tried to do to you. Sex is enjoyable, it's a fun release, and it should never be used as a weapon against someone."

I was glad he saw it that way, as that's how I thought of it too. "You know all about my personal life. Tell me something about yours now too."

Monroe gave me a shrewd look before he continued to eat the hunk of cheese he was holding between his fingers. "What is it that you'd like to know?"

I shrugged and took a sip of wine. It was dark and fruity, not that I knew much about wine. It wasn't something a lot of people drank where I came from. We weren't that refined.

"Relationships?"

"A few. Nothing serious since I began Asiq. It's hard to think of something long-term when everyone around me seems interested in getting something out of me rather than actually in me, if that makes sense. Even you."

That caught me off guard. "No, I wasn't."

He lifted a single dark eyebrow as if to challenge me on that. "Really? The only reason you came back to have sex with Dragonfly each time was because you were paid. Exceptionally well, I might add. If you'd been patient enough to make your time with Dragonfly last longer, you could have retired on that money alone."

I didn't have a good comeback for that, since it was the truth, but only part of it. "I came back each time because I was in love, not because of the money. If you wanted to again sometime, I wouldn't ask for anything, just no mask."

He watched me for a long time after that. I kept eating. "Would you insist on faithfulness, or are you expecting the sex to be about fun and mutual release?"

"I would demand it, yes." I wasn't going to negotiate with him, or anyone else about that.

"How would you go about trusting me, then, given where I live and who I'm around all night and day?"

I knew it wouldn't be easy. There were a lot of good-looking guys, not just in Asiq but on Wish in general. "It would take some time."

141

Monroe tipped his head toward me and took a long sip of wine before asking me his next question. "And, assuming we did manage to make it through the next two years of your training, being a pilot will take you away for long periods of time. How will you handle that?"

Finally an answer that was easy and one I had ready for him. "I'd take system jobs to stay close. We could see each other all the time then."

Monroe shook his head and sighed loudly. "It's always the prettiest ones who are the stupidest."

I bristled instantly. "What's that supposed to mean exactly?" I demanded.

He sat his wineglass down and placed his hands flat on the table in front of him. "It means you should never, ever, give up on something you really want for the sake of someone else. You want to use jump gates?" I nodded. He knew I did. "Then you cannot take system jobs, so don't even suggest such a thing."

I shook my head angrily and tried not to snap at him, but I was quickly losing control of my emotions. And he was still so damn calm. "I'd do it for love. Because I loved you when you were Dragonfly, and maybe I could even love you again now that I know who you are. Eventually. If you weren't such a jerk sometimes."

"You would be stupid to give up something for love," he retorted, making love sound like a dirty word as it fell from his lips.

I knew he was wrong. "Love is worth it. Always. People do amazing, wonderful things for love. I was reading about this place in class. A man built a city to keep his wife safe. Because he loved her."

Monroe rolled his eyes. "Waste of recourses and time."

"I don't agree with you," I snapped.

Monroe pushed himself back from the table and started to stand up. "Well, this was enlightening, at least. It's late, and I'm far too tired to play games with idealistic, naive children."

He wasn't going to be able to dismiss me that easily, especially not after he'd just insulted me too. "Why did you pay that much for me to begin with if you weren't interested? You could have let someone else win the auction. I saw the other bids. There were plenty. You didn't have to be Dragonfly."

"I was interested in you, Thierry. I'd never had a virgin, especially one of your kind. I knew, after seeing you open up to me, the experience would likely be intoxicating, and you didn't disappoint me. Falling in love with you wasn't supposed to happen, but it did, and it was a mistake. Clearly you aren't mature enough to love someone."

My wineglass was in my hand and flying across the table at him before he'd even finished speaking.

CHAPTER THIRTEEN

WITH WINE running down his chest and soaking through his expensive looking shirt, he grabbed my arm before I could get more than a few feet away from the table. I'd expected him to be angry, but I hadn't expected him to wrap his arms around me and press his mouth fiercely against mine. I moaned against his lips as he shoved his tongue into my mouth, and suddenly it was like there'd been no time lost between us. I could feel a bit of his shadowy beard against my cheek and it made me shiver. He reached down to cup my butt through my pants. When he moved his hands to my outer thighs, I jumped up against his hips, and he caught me and carried me over to the bed. I was angry with him, but I also wanted him so very much too.

It made no sense to me, and if I'd actually stopped to think about it, I would have told him no. And he would have stopped and let me go. But I didn't want to stop. I wanted him as he was, just like that. I shuddered as he rubbed against me through our clothes and kissed his neck while I tore open his shirt so I could get my hands on his chest and to his ribs, where I could see his tattoo.

Monroe moved back and flipped me over so I was facedown on the bed with him behind me and pressing against my butt. I'd wanted to be able to see him, but I also liked him like this and really, I was getting him again, so it didn't exactly matter how that got accomplished. I stopped thinking so much as I opened up every nerve in my body and just let myself feel. If this was my one time with Monroe as he really was, if this was the last time I'd get to be with the man I loved, then I wasn't going to hold back.

He reached around to the front of my pants and, after getting them open in only a few short seconds, yanked them down over my butt and to my thighs, exposing me. I'd never not been naked in this room before, and having sex with him while still keeping some of my clothes on was somehow even hotter than being completely exposed to him.

I curled my fingers into the sheet as he began to stretch me. It'd been so long, far too long, to deny ourselves this.

He tangled his fingers in my hair, holding my head still as he bent over my back and bit into my shoulder. "Tell me what you want," he nearly growled.

I knew what he was asking because I remembered his reaction to the one time I'd said it to him. "Fuck me, please," I nearly begged, and then I was crying out as he pushed his way into me. The pain, the discomfort, didn't last long before the heat inside me took over, and I was sliding back to meet him each time as if we'd always been doing this and hadn't spent weeks apart. He let go of my hair to wrap an arm around my chest and hold me close, and I gasped through each wonderful moment with him.

Monroe panted in my ear. He whispered how good I felt, how much he'd missed me, and I agreed with him each time. We were good like that, with only the sex between us, and thankfully being with him made the rest of it, all our complications, melt away.

But having him in me felt too good to last for long, and once he took me in his hand, it was over far too quickly. I spilled over the sheets, and he emptied himself within me, and we were done. The moment was gone, and we were thrust back into reality with cruel force. He lay down beside me, and we struggled to catch our breaths.

"Great sex doesn't mean I forgive you," I stubbornly said, getting up as soon as I could manage without falling over, and started cleaning myself up.

Monroe laughed and shook his head. "You couldn't let the moment last for five more minutes, could you? If you want to stay angry, that's too bad for you. A grudge is a hard thing to hold on to."

I was grateful I hadn't managed to get my shirt too dirty, and put myself away before turning back to him. He hadn't bothered to fix his clothes at all, and I couldn't keep my eyes off him.

"And it had nothing to do with love," I added. I wasn't a child, I wasn't naive, and hot sex wouldn't change me being hurt over what he'd said.

Monroe sat up. It was as if he didn't care we had been in the middle of an argument, and the moment for sex had passed with the return of my temper. "That kind of sex rarely does."

That made me pause. "What do you mean by that?"

"Do you want to know?" he asked. I nodded. "Do you want to be shown?"

"I do." He was teasing me and wouldn't actually do anything. But then he reached for me, and I let him lead me to a clean spot on the big bed. I lay down on my back, and he lay on his side.

"Lift your head. Rest it on my arm," he told me, which I did. He put his hand on my cheek, looked down into my eyes, and gave me a gentle kiss. Then he put one of his legs over mine, and I rested my hand on his outer thigh.

I was still pretty sure he wouldn't do anything. Except that he undid my pants, then slipped his hand over me while he continued to kiss me and hold my face still with his hand.

It was slow, and it was wonderful as he held me and gave me pleasure with no regard to his own. I couldn't tell if he wanted to go again, but he didn't do anything more than give me another release after he'd pushed up my shirt to keep it clean. I arched up as far as his leg over mine would allow, and when I came crashing back down, he continued to kiss me gently as I emptied myself on my stomach and over his hand.

He held me without saying a single word as I caught my breath and came back to myself. And when he released me just long enough to clean me up with a warm, damp washcloth before giving me a kiss on my cheek, I was nearly ready to cry.

"Why do you have to hurt me so much?" I mumbled as I fixed my pants.

Monroe shook his head and joined me on the bed. I sat down next to him with our backs against the headboard. "I never intended to hurt you, Thierry. I honestly never thought it would get this far. When I bid on you, I only wanted a little of your beauty for myself. I took a chance on asking if you'd come back for a visit, never expecting you to say yes. But when you did, I was thrilled. And then I couldn't stop asking you, because I wanted more of you each time." He took a deep breath and looked down at his hands. "Can you forgive me for my deception? And for what I asked your brother to say to you?"

"It'll be hard," I admitted.

"Holding on to negativity will hurt you more in the long run. Believe me. I'm speaking from experience."

I pulled my knees to my chest and hugged them. "Sometimes I wish you'd never bid on me. Things could have been simpler that way. They would have been. I think anyone else would have left me alone after that. I would have been used, and I would have taken what I needed from them too, and that would have been the end of it."

Monroe nodded and reached over to hold one of my hands in his. "I sometimes wish your brother had never introduced us. Then maybe I could sleep at night instead of lying awake thinking about you or not look up at the door every time it opens, hoping that it might be you."

I was quiet for a long time after that. "Things were better when you were Dragonfly to me. Life wasn't nearly as complicated. It was easy to love you, want you, need you in my life. I used to look forward to seeing you each month, like that was the only thing there was for me, like I had to be with you, and the time was never long enough for me."

"Those times were easier, but I doubt they were all that much better. I'm sorry, Thierry, but I have work to do now. And your brother is likely done with his client and wondering what is taking you so long to have dinner."

I nodded, knowing he was probably right. "Wait, one more question?"

"Yes?"

I frowned as I tried to think of a question that might keep him there with me, since I hadn't actually had one ready. But I couldn't come up with a good enough one, so I asked him something to allay my curiosity instead.

"What is it you do all day here, anyway?"

He smiled and gave my hand a squeeze. "What is it that you think I do?"

I smiled back and laid my head on his shoulder. He turned to kiss me on my head. "I assume you're not constantly having sex with all the guys here all the time."

"No. I'm not doing that. Since you came into my office, I haven't been doing that at all, though that wasn't always the case. I'm sure some of the men here think I've taken a new vow of celibacy or something equally unfitting to my profession. I doubt any of them have guessed I've actually fallen in love."

He didn't give me any time to respond to that, so I basked in the knowledge that at one time, when we'd been great together, he had loved me. And I'd loved him too, and for a while things had been perfect. There's no way it could have lasted, I knew that now, but months ago I'd thought I could have hung on to that moment forever and never let it go. I should have clung tighter.

"Much of my day is spent talking to clients, organizing events, listening to my employees, and trying to help them with their problems. The people that come here, both clients and employees, know what to expect. I don't get a lot of turnover because I run one of the best places on the planet, and my clients are never a problem because they know they won't find better service than in this establishment. Are you done with the questions?"

I knew I was being dismissed, and yet I couldn't get my feet to move. I couldn't understand why sometimes I hated him, wanted nothing to do with him, and wished I'd never met him or had the idea to sell my virginity. And then other times, I was left feeling like he somehow fit into my life, like there might be a place for him there, so I had to leave a little room for him. I wasn't an incomplete puzzle needing some missing piece. I was someone who knew what love was and believed I had found it. It was hard for me to walk away from that so easily.

"For now," I told him.

"Then good night, Thierry. I'll be in my office if you need me for something. I'm fairly certain you won't, though." He got up and left me alone in the room.

I'd been pretty sure I wasn't going to go to him again that night, but that conviction only lasted an hour until I was back at the door to his office and quietly knocking on it.

"Come in, Thierry," he called through the door. "Back so soon?" he asked me as I came in and closed the door behind me.

I sat down across from him at his desk. "I had more questions."

Monroe smirked and went back to looking at the holoscreen in his hands. "Of course you did. Mind if I work while I answer them?"

"I'd like to have your full attention," I stubbornly said.

When he looked at me, he appeared to be surprised at my nerve, but also a bit annoyed as well. "Then you'll have to make an appointment. I have some availability next week."

I huffed irritably. "You know I can't come back then. I'm only free one weekend a month, then I'm there the rest of the time."

He slid the holoscreen aside, giving me the attention I'd asked for. I fidgeted under his gaze until I put my hands in front of me on his desk in an attempt to stop myself from picking at the arms of the chair.

"With so little free time, I would assume you'd want to be with your brother," he said.

"He's with a client." Corbin hadn't told me that exactly, but I was pretty sure he was occupied with someone right then.

Monroe frowned and pulled his holoscreen in front of him again. I was about to protest when I noticed the different camera views he was flipping through before he put it aside again.

"No, he isn't. If he's preoccupied with someone in his room, then he's doing it on his own time."

That didn't make any sense. "But—"

Monroe wasn't budging. "I assure you, Thierry, I know where my clients are at all times when they are here, and your brother isn't with anyone at this moment. But I'm fairly certain you didn't come to talk to me about your brother's sex life. Did you?"

"No, of course not," I quickly told him.

Monroe nodded and pressed his fingers together to form a little tent in front of him on the desk. "Great. Then what is it, and please make it quick."

I took a deep breath and chose one question at random out of the hundreds currently circling my brain. "Do you know how to be monogamous?"

"Are you expecting monogamy from someone that has tempting men around him at all times?" Monroe asked me with a raised brow.

I pursed my lips. Of course I knew where he lived and who he was around, but he could have been a little nicer to me about it. "I just thought—"

Monroe shook his head and placed his palms flat on his desk. "You thought you could take what we had when I was Dragonfly and somehow make it work in this context? Is that what I'm getting from you right now? I realize this may come as a shock to you, but things can't be as simple as you would like them to be between us. You can't hate me for not telling you I was Dragonfly, then also ask if I'm able to commit to you. Make up your mind, Thierry."

I didn't know what to say to that. He was right, I knew he was. And yet he'd been so blunt about it, needlessly so. "I stopped hating you a long time ago," I mumbled.

Monroe sighed. "What are you doing here? Honestly?"

I couldn't tell what he was thinking. He seemed tired, but if that was because of me or his job, I had no way of knowing. I was trying to figure this out, and I needed his help, but I didn't want to piss him off by getting it either.

"I'm trying to see if there's any hope for us or if I should walk away and call it a life lesson not to trust people again. You hurt me. Can't you see that?"

Monroe's expression softened a little, and I tried to force myself to relax. I loved him. I didn't have to be so on edge around him. Things would be okay somehow. I had to believe that for it to come true.

"I do see that. But I can't fix it. I've explained why I couldn't tell you I was Dragonfly, and now it's up to you to either accept what happened and move on or get stuck in a web of blaming me and feeling hurt about it. We had fun, you and I. There's no reason that should be tainted by your feelings of betrayal."

He was wrong, and I'd make him see that. At least I'd try to. "I choose option three," I told him.

Monroe shook his head and leaned back in his chair, putting more distance between us. "There is no third option. You only get two choices here."

I grinned at him, because I was right and he'd see that soon enough. "No, wrong. You only think there are two choices."

"Fine, enlighten me. What is the third choice?" He rolled his eyes and waved a hand at me, as if telling me to continue.

"You consider a relationship with me where we are both honest with each other. No one will ever know that you were the man who bid on me. I've promised you that. But I'll need to know you aren't having sex with guys while I'm away most of the month."

It was a simple request, one I was hoping he'd grant me. He was worth it to me, and I needed to know I was worth it for him too.

He surprised me with his next question. "How do I know you won't be having sex with the boys you go to school with?"

I groaned and rubbed my hands through my hair in frustration. "Because I'm sitting here asking you to be faithful. I wouldn't be having sex with them and asking you not to have sex on the side too. I'm not a hypocrite," I nearly snapped.

Monroe stared at me. "No, just an idealistic child."

It took me a minute or two to figure out what that meant, coming from him. And when I got it, the realization that he didn't want me, at all, hurt more than I'd thought possible. "Then you won't do it? You won't even take a chance?"

He laughed at me, but there was no happiness in the sound, only pain. "On what? You running off after the first shiny thing that happens to catch your attention? Boys your age are such magpies."

"Mag whats?" I had no idea what he was talking about.

"Magpies. They are a bird from old Earth. They were small and.... Oh, never mind."

"I won't run off," I promised him. I was sure of it, because I knew myself, and even though I'd never been in love before, I was certain I wouldn't ruin this with Monroe, if only he'd be willing to try to repair things between us. We hadn't fallen so much that we were unfixable. I didn't think so at least.

Monroe shook his head, then crossed his arms. To me it looked like he was barricading himself because there was no way I was getting through to him at all that night. "Oh, to be young and so self-assured of what you feel and what you're capable of."

It sounded like he was mocking me, and I narrowed my eyes at him. "And you, old man, are so set in your ways, you're not even willing to take a chance on finding love."

He glared right back, but he did unfold his arms long enough to smack his hands on the desk between us as he got up. "I had love with you, boy, and you chose to run as soon as you saw who I was. Am I supposed to think you won't do the exact same thing again?"

"I thought you had sex with my brother!" I nearly shouted at him as I got up too so I could face him without him looming over me.

"You trusted Dragonfly. Why am I so different?" Monroe demanded.

"You run a brothel." It wasn't a good answer, not in the least. But it was the first thing that popped into my mind, and I let it fall out of my mouth. Looking back, it probably wasn't the best idea I'd ever had.

He snorted and shook his head as if he couldn't believe what I'd just said, and honestly I didn't know why I had either. Asiq was more than a brothel, it was an experience as Monroe liked to remind me, and my brother worked here. That made it something special and made Monroe something different, something more, than the typical kind of man I thought would run a brothel.

"You trusted Dragonfly not to have sex with anyone else, didn't you? Never mind. Don't answer that. I can guess your answer well enough. And Dragonfly could have run an interstellar drug smuggling ring. You had no reason to trust him except that you wanted to. My establishment is legal, well kept, and makes far more money than you could ever dream of. I think we're done here. Get out of my office."

I wasn't ready to go. "But—"

Monroe shook his head, showing me he could be just as hard-headed and stubborn as me. "Unless the next words out of your mouth are asking me to take off my pants and fuck you, we really are done here."

"I—" Nothing immediately came to mind.

Monroe pointed at the door as if I'd forgotten where it was. "Don't make me throw you out, little boy. I'm bigger and stronger than you. Don't think I won't make you go."

"Won't you take off your pants and fuck me?"

Monroe rolled his eyes and dropped his hand down on the desk. "You don't actually mean that." He sounded almost hopeful, and if he'd wanted me to have sex with him, I wouldn't have said no.

I would have enjoyed it, would have begged him for more, and still been left feeling frustrated and confused, like I was now. I shook my head. "No, I don't. But I don't want to go either."

Monroe gave me a little smile, and for a moment there, I thought he was going to kiss me, or at the very least hug me, but he didn't. He didn't even lift a hand to touch me.

"Sometimes you don't get what you want. Actually, most times you won't. If anyone ever told you that you did, they were lying to you. Here's some free advice, kid: sex is easy, relationships are hard, and grumpy old men don't have relationships with boys."

I was so very tired of him treating me like a child that I snapped at him. "Maybe they do, and maybe they don't. Maybe that's just your excuse for why you'll fuck me and tell me you love me until your mask comes off."

Monroe gave me a level stare as his smile grew into something wicked. "Don't you remember? I've fucked you without the mask on too. And you loved it. Don't pretend you wouldn't let me take you right here on this desk if I wanted to. I've got half a mind to do just that. Maybe it'll rid you of some of your ridiculous notions."

I wasn't going to let him know how right he was. My blush was doing that plenty without my help. "I loved you too. I could again. If you weren't so damn stubborn and plain old mean."

Monroe nearly groaned. "Grow up, and once again, get out of my office."

I tossed up my hands in frustration and started toward the door. "Fine. I'm going. You don't have to be so cruel. I could hate you just fine without you being like that."

"Good. Then do it, if that's your choice. Just go."

I rolled my eyes and took another step toward the door. "Would be nice to be given a choice to hate you or not. You seem convinced it only has to be one way and are unwilling to consider anything else."

Monroe held up his hand, and I stopped walking, waiting for him to say something, anything that would get me to stay there with him. I doubted it was possible. Not that there wasn't something that would have made me want to run back into his arms. I could think of a dozen of those easily without even trying. But I doubted he would have used a single one. He was mad at me, and I was angry at him right back, but I only got this one weekend a month to see him, and there was so much I couldn't get with him on a com call.

"What is it you think you want? Exactly," he said, his voice level.

"What I want is to have my Dragonfly back." I realized I sounded like a petulant child wanting their favorite toy again the moment the words came out of my mouth, but there wasn't anything I could do about that once they were there between us.

"Too bad. You're stuck with me," he replied coldly.

"Then I want you to love me like you did." I was nearly shaking as I snapped at him. Reasoning with Monroe was starting to feel like a lost cause, and I hated that I'd let my heart get so heavily involved. It seemed like this had been nothing more than a convenient way for him to get some sex. Though honestly, it hadn't been all that convenient or cheap. I hated that he seemed to be throwing what we had, and me, away so easily without fighting for it, like I was trying to.

He gave me a long, hard look. "In exchange for what?" he asked as if this was some simple business arrangement and not love.

"Me," I replied simply.

He looked like he wanted to laugh, as if he didn't think I was being serious. But then he stopped himself and simply shook his head. "All one hundred and sixty pounds of bitterness and hate that you are right now? No, thank you."

"If you'll agree to try, then I will too." I forced the words out quickly before I could second-guess myself, before I could give up as easily as he'd seemed to and just walk away from him and what we'd had now. He seemed to want me the least now, when I knew that he was all I wanted. I loved him, and I wanted to throw one of his expensive looking vases at his head for being as stupid as he was being in that moment.

"Or what?"

I was beyond trying to reason with him, but still I stood there for some stupid reason, as if I had nowhere else to go. "Do you need to threaten me?" I was tired of this game, tired of feeling like I was pushing him and ending up against a cold steel wall. I loved him when he was Dragonfly, and I'd enjoyed having sex with him when he was Monroe. Somewhere in there I knew there was a middle ground. I just had to find it while I still had his attention.

"Is there anything else that would work on you?"

I rolled my eyes. There was a vase in the corner on a nice-looking black stand that seemed like a good piece to chuck at his head. I was getting pretty tempted. "Try being nice. Just once. You were so good to me before." I shouldn't have sounded like I was pleading, begging him to notice me, take me back. I wished he'd stop acting like a complete and utter jerk.

"Oh, is that what you thought was happening? You were paid to enjoy sex. Let's not pretend it was anything else." His eye twitched, and I didn't know what it meant, but I knew it was significant.

"You told me you loved me," I pressed, even as I moved back against the door. I wondered if the people in the hallway could hear us talking. We weren't yelling, not anymore at least, but we were so frustrated with each other we weren't exactly hiding our conversation, either.

Monroe nodded. "And so did you. But people who love each other, they don't run the first time something bad happens."

"You think that's what I did?" I asked.

"I know it was."

I'd hit my limit of him for the night. "Fine. Then I guess we're over."

Monroe shrugged, as if my words didn't matter to him at all. I didn't believe that for a second, though. "Don't fall for your own delusions. We never had anything but a business arrangement."

Fine, if he wanted to play things that way, I could do that too. I slipped off the bracelet and tossed it on the floor between us. "Here's your bracelet back."

He didn't move to get it. I didn't think he even looked at it. "Okay. Don't forget where the door is."

"Oh, I won't."

"Good."

"Bye." Some part of me still wanted him to tell me not to go, despite everything. I wanted to strangle that little bit of me.

He nodded toward the door behind me. "Still waiting for you to get out of my office and let me get back to work."

"Won't be waiting long."

"And yet you're still standing there. Get out, or I will make you. You're a stubborn, idiotic, insolent child, and I—"

I slammed the door behind me, leaving him alone in his big office with his unbroken vase that I really regretted not breaking over his head.

CHAPTER FOURTEEN

AS SOON as I was back at the academy the next night, I transferred all the credits I'd saved back into Monroe's account. I'd spent most of what he'd given me on tuition, and after that I'd bought some clothes and other things, but a good chunk of it was still there.

I did it because I didn't want his money. Because what I'd had with Dragonfly after the first time had been about love and not about being Monroe's personal whore whenever he felt like having a good screw. I hated him for tainting what I'd seen as wonderful, and if I would have had any chance at being a pilot without going to school, I would have gotten a refund for that too and sent it all to him before going back to the apartment I shared with Corbin.

I was in a bad mood most of that first week, but it got really bad in combat training. I was with Mr. Allessan again, because of course no one would go against me. It was like I had some form of fatal disease I could pass on to them just by trying to hurt them in one of the three heavily padded places we were allowed to kick each other.

I'd struck out and hit Mr. Allessan's outer thigh when I got knocked down by something hard from the side. I fell and grabbed my head as some girl bent over me. "Are you okay? Thierry?"

"No, don't touch him!" one girl cried out.

"And don't let him touch you either!" a boy added on.

I rolled my eyes and got to my knees, which hurt. My head felt like it was broken open, but I still managed to get up. Mr. Allessan put a hand around my side, then quickly pulled back.

"You won't tell Monroe if I help you to the medic, will you?"

I shook my head, and even though I hadn't said anything, that seemed to be good enough for him. He dropped me off in the medic's office, and after a lot of tests, I was told I couldn't go back to class that day, and I couldn't do any combat training or running for at least a week. Before, I might have rejoiced at that news. But all it let me do was have more time to sulk.

That night I heard from Monroe. I figured it was coming, since I'd done such a large transfer, and was prepared to brush off anything he had to say. But I couldn't delete the note without reading it first.

Why is so much of my money back?

That was easy enough to answer. *Because I felt like it.*

My com unit came to life, and I picked up the call, already knowing it was him. "Yes?"

"I want an honest answer, Thierry. Why is all that money back? Are you quitting school? Are you giving up on everything you wanted? I demand to know."

I rolled my eyes and lay back on my bed. "I demand you stop snapping in my ear." I had a headache after being punched in the head by a girl who'd misjudged her opponent, and Monroe wasn't helping my situation one bit.

"What's wrong with you? You sound like you're in pain." He had at least softened his tone for my benefit.

I put a hand over my eyes to block out some of the bright light. Even though I had the overhead lights off, the sunlight came through the windows across from me. "That's probably because I am in pain."

"What happened?"

"Combat training."

"Thierry...."

159

I sighed. "Monroe, I'm fine. Really. I have to take it easy for a little while, and I have an excuse to get out of a few physical classes. Not a big deal. Anything else, or are we done here?" I was nearly parroting back our conversation from earlier. I hoped he'd get the connection.

"I expected you to have spent that money as soon as you got it."

I rolled my eyes. "Guess you misjudged me, because I was saving it for something, but I'll find another way to get it now."

"What were you saving for?"

I couldn't tell if he was genuinely curious or just making conversation. Since I'd never known Monroe to spare a moment to end up wasting it, I figured he actually wanted to know. So I spared him the games and told him the truth. "If it matters...."

"It does."

I rolled onto my side to get away from the bright sunlight. "I was saving up for a shuttle of my own. Most of the people in my classes already have one from their parents. I want one too. Corbin has his, and I could borrow it sometimes, but I'm going to need one at some point to go between worlds, especially when I start really doing internships and bouncing all over the place."

Monroe took a few minutes to answer me, but before he did, all the money I'd transferred to him had been sent right back to my account. "Keep it. We had a business arrangement, and each transaction was completed. You held up your end of the bargain. It's only fair you keep the money you earned."

I wasn't going to argue with him about it if he didn't want to have it. "Thank you. Yes, it was a business transaction. Anything else?"

"No. Do you need anything there?"

"I don't." That was a lie. I needed him. But I wasn't about to say that again. He'd already rejected me a few too many times for me to come crawling back to him, begging for more.

"Okay. Good-bye."

"Bye." I hung up the call as quickly as I could and tried to relax until I knew my roommates would come looking for me, wondering where I was. We were close enough now that I was pretty sure I could count on them to do that when I'd been kicked in the head.

It was another week before I heard anything from Monroe. I was surprised to hear from him again so soon actually, but I was glad of it too. I missed him. I had a virtual stack of started notes, telling him just that, and I never planned to send off any of them.

> *Thierry,*
> *I have an associate looking for an apprentice on*
> *a science transport ship, I realize you won't be ready*
> *for something like this until you've graduated, but*
> *would you like me to pass along your information to*
> *the captain in case he has an opening in a few years?*
> *Monroe*

Being an apprentice wasn't the same thing as being a copilot, but it would get me experience. And I thought it was nice he was still trying to look out for me. I knew he still cared, and I didn't know why he wouldn't try.

> *Monroe,*
> *Please give him my contact information. Thank you.*
> *Thierry*

I sent the letter off, but as I stared down at my holoscreen, I wanted to say more, so I started another one.

> *I'm sorry I screamed when I took off your mask*
> *and had sex with someone else to hurt you.*

As far as apologies went, it was a horrible one, and I could have said so much more, but I didn't know how to go about saying any of it. My com started ringing, and I put the earpiece in my ear as

I stood up from the bench I was sitting on and started to walk along the path that went around the academy.

"Hello?" I was reasonably sure who it was since the call had come seconds after I'd sent off the note.

"Hi."

I smiled. "Hey." It was good to hear his voice again, to not be fighting, to not be standing in front of him stuck somewhere between wanting to cry and wanting to scream at him.

"I'm sorry I put my business concerns above yours in my deception."

I'd needed to hear him say that, but at the same time, I got it. "Your business comes first. I understand."

I heard something that I thought was a bed squeak, and I found myself getting instantly jealous at the idea of him being in bed with someone else.

"Were you just having sex?" I blurted as I tried to get hold of my anger.

Monroe laughed. "You hear me get out of bed and think it's because I'm having sex?"

I didn't know what to think, actually. "You don't owe me anything. It's not as if we're together." Those words really hurt to say.

"No, we're not. But I still care about you. Deeply. And I can't have sex with someone while I feel this way about you. That's not fair to them."

I sighed and found a little patch of shade under a big tree to sit down under. "Like I did? I hate thinking about that night, about what happened between us and what I did. It wasn't fair, and it was stupid."

"You sound so much more reasonable when you're in a completely different system."

I smiled, because he was right. "It's easy to have a clear head when you're not in front of me, jumbling everything up. I can barely think around you, and then you're so stubborn that I...." I shook my head. "I don't want to fight with you. Not again. I wanted to apologize for what I did back then."

"Thank you. It was hard to watch."

"Because of how much you loved me?" I asked him hopefully.

"Yes, but also because you were hurting yourself. You may have wanted to get back at me, and you did, but I saw your face, and I saw how miserable you were. I wanted to rush down there and save you from yourself, but I was so sure you were done with me for good."

I wiped at my eyes and brought my knees up to my chest. "I was sure of that too. But I couldn't stay away."

"Neither could I."

"Friends?" I asked him hopefully.

Monroe chuckled. "Is that what you really want?"

"No." It would be much too little, but I didn't know what else we could have.

"Neither do I, and I can't see either of us actually happy with that sort of arrangement. You always feel too far away, but when I have you right in front of me, it's as if I can't begin to talk to you."

I laughed. "I feel the same way. I want to yell at you, but I also just want you too."

"We make a fine pair, you and I."

I didn't deny it, because sometimes I thought we still had half a chance, but I knew it would take a lot of work too. A few people passed by me on the path and waved to me. I waved back while I thought of something to say to him.

I licked my lips and went out on a limb. "What's keeping you from wanting me for more than sex?" I asked him bluntly.

Monroe took his time answering me, and I was about to laugh it off and say some sort of stupid joke or something to let him know his answer wasn't needed, didn't matter, and I wasn't being serious. Only I was, and it did matter to me, a lot.

"Will you come see me on your next weekend off?" he asked instead of giving me the answer I was hoping for.

There was no question in my mind, I would be there. "Yes. Arrange it for me again please?"

"I'm not your travel service," Monroe replied, though I knew he was smiling, because I could hear it in his voice.

I smiled too, even as my nervousness made me uneasy. "Please? You do a better job at it than I do." I didn't know what he wanted to say to me that he couldn't over the com, but I was looking forward to seeing him again.

"Fine. Be ready to go early, as usual."

"I always am."

He laughed at that. "I need to get back to work. Thank you for taking my call."

He didn't need to say that to me. "I'll always take them."

"Be safe out there."

"Don't fall in love with someone else before I get there," I told him. I was joking, and I didn't even know why I'd said it, but I heard the hitch in his voice. We spent so much time apart, and I wasn't the most attractive, nicest, smartest, or sexiest guy he saw every day.

Monroe sounded completely serious when he replied. "That wouldn't happen. Loving you takes up far too much energy for this old man as it is."

"You're not that old. Stop playing."

He'd said he had to go, and if he'd insisted, I would have let him. But if he wanted to keep talking to me, I still had some time, and I'd gladly keep him on the phone for as long as I could.

"I'm forty-three, double your age and then some," he told me as if it hurt him.

I shrugged. It was a big gap, and some people might have had a problem with it, but I wasn't one of them. "I can't change our age difference, so I don't see why that's a problem."

"You are so stubborn."

"So are you."

He laughed. "Yes, I suppose I am. And there's something we have in common. I will see you when you get here."

"Yes, you will. Bye." It was a promise, and I'd be keeping it because we needed to talk to each other in person. I wouldn't yell at him, and he wouldn't throw me out, not this time. I'd make sure of it.

I hung up and pulled my earpiece out of my ear as I smiled at the thought of seeing Monroe again.

CORBIN NEARLY tackled me as soon as I came into Asiq. No one asked who I was anymore. They all assumed I was there to see my brother. And they were half right. "Hey!" I said when he let me have enough space to breathe again.

As before, he took my bag from me and led me into the room next to his. "Hey. You look good. Taller even. Did you grow on me while you were away?"

"It's only been two months!" I laughed as I fell back on the bed. It was so good to stretch out again after being in small shuttles and crammed into transport ships. I looked at the camera on the wall and wondered if Monroe was watching me even now. He probably was. I gave him a quick wave while Corbin's back was to me.

"You know, I think you did a number on Monroe," he said as he sat down next to me.

I frowned. "Why?"

Corbin shrugged. "Nothing too major. Just little things I've noticed. Like him being an asshole a lot more than usual. He was always a tough boss, but that's what made this place great to work at, because he's fair too. But lately he's been a little snappy. The guys think he's stressed about something. I think he misses you."

I rolled my eyes. "Even if he did, we're not great together. We argue as soon as we get in the room. When we're not—" I shut my mouth tightly before I could finish that thought.

"You think I don't know you have sex with him?" Corbin laughed and lay down on his side next to me. "And yeah, that's a bit of a head trip too."

165

"You almost sound like you're okay with it. With us being together, if there ever was an *us* before or in the future."

Corbin made a face, and I knew I had missed something. "I don't love it. I mean, he's a lot older than you. But I've been thinking, and you're older than I was when I fell in love with the guy I was telling you about. And yes, he's your first love, and yes, that can be disastrous. But at the same time, maybe you're old enough to figure out for yourself who you want. Maybe it's okay for you to make mistakes sometimes." He turned to look at me, and I gave him a weak smile as I reached up to touch his hand. "You were so young when our parents died, and I've felt like I've been raising you. I just want you to be okay. If he makes you happy, then maybe I can deal with that. And since he's here, I can make sure he stays in line when it comes to you."

I gave his hand a squeeze. "I know you're worried, and you did a great job taking over. But you don't have to be my parent and my brother anymore. You can just be my brother. You're not responsible for me. You don't have to do that for me anymore."

He nodded and then wrapped me in a big hug. We lay like that for a long time, as we had the night our parents died in the accident. I'd been so scared, so worried about what was going to happen to us. But he'd stepped up and taken care of me, and he hadn't stopped for a minute.

"I think you should call the guy who left you," I told him after a while.

"That came out of nowhere." He sounded like he was about to fall asleep. I elbowed him in the ribs, since I knew he had to get up and go to his client in a little bit.

"I'm serious. You should."

Corbin shrugged. "Probably not. But why?"

I rolled over in his arms so I could face him. "Because he hurt you, and he's an idiot, and you never got over him."

"So your solution is for me to call him, have him probably not remember me at all, and then me to get hurt all over again? No, thank you."

"Or have him completely remember you, been missing you this whole time and feeling horrible for what he did, and then for you to hang up on him," I offered.

Corbin's face lit up with his big grin. "Yeah. That kind of payback would be nice."

I nodded and sat up. "Good. You think about it."

"Where you going?" he asked as I got off the bed and took off my academy jacket, hanging it up on the hook on the wall.

"To see Monroe. And you need to go get ready for your client. Your breath needs some work." We still had time, but I wanted to see him while I was thinking about Corbin reconnecting with someone he'd once loved. Maybe it would be good for him to do it, maybe not. But he had to try, just like I did.

Corbin threw a pillow at me, hitting me in the back of the head before I could get out the door. I found Monroe's office door open and slipped inside before he noticed me.

"You're early. I didn't expect you for another hour," he said as he looked up at me. I shut the door behind me before crossing to his desk. I could have sat down in the chair across from him, but instead I went around to the front and sat down on the edge of his desk. He lifted his eyebrows, and I didn't budge.

"I'm here now."

He smirked. "I can see that."

I wanted to touch him, but I didn't try to. I was hoping he'd touch me, though.

"Classes are good?" he asked.

"They are. I did well on my midterms. Finals are coming up. It's been almost a year since I started." Which meant I'd been in love with Monroe, as either Dragonfly or himself, for that long too.

He seemed to completely miss what I was saying, and the significance of it between us, as he said, "That's nice. Is there anything you need?"

"To talk to you."

Monroe gestured for me to continue. "So talk. I'm fortunately between appointments at the moment. I can give you ten minutes at most."

That wouldn't be nearly enough time, but I understood he was busy, and I'd make the most of the time he was giving me. "I want to try again."

"Try what?"

"Us," I replied, as if that should have been obvious.

He quickly shook his head. "No."

"Why not?" If he was going to say something ridiculous again about how I was a child, I was going to…. No. I hadn't come here to argue with him or yell or stomp around and slam his door, like I had last time. I could listen to his reasons, even though they were going to be wrong, and then counter them with my own.

"Because what I will ask you for, you will not want." His words surprised me, because there wasn't anything he could have asked me for I wouldn't have instantly given him.

"And what is that?" I asked him with a frown.

He looked incredibly sad as he stared up at me, and I wished I could have done something to ease that pain. "I want you to leave this place and only come back after you've seen all the worlds you possibly can. I want you to go explore, become a pilot, do everything you've ever wanted with your life, and then, and only then, if you still want a relationship with me after seeing everything every solar system has to offer, then I will say yes to you. But I will not take your future, and I will not take the love of someone who does not know what it means to give it. You want me, those are my terms."

Tears pricked at my eyes as I struggled to grasp at anything to say that would counter his proposal. "I will still need to see my brother," I finally managed to get out.

Monroe nodded. "Of course. I will change his schedule to match your school one so that you can visit him at your home. He won't know why." I didn't correct him in his thinking that Corbin didn't know about us. He'd been good at keeping my secret, and I didn't want to give Monroe another reason to be mad at me, especially one that could lead to Corbin losing his job at Asiq.

My bottom lip started to tremble. "I want to hear from you still."

Monroe reached over and put his hand on my thigh. "Then write letters. We were always better in our letters."

He was right, we always were. But that still didn't mean I wanted to agree with him, even though a little voice in the back of my mind was telling me he was right and this would be the best thing for us. I wanted to fight against that idea, to scream that we were good right now, right here in this moment. But even though we were, this wasn't how we normally were, and I knew we would have work to do, and we couldn't have a relationship, not a real one anyway, with a whole system between us. I wiped at my eyes to stop the tears, but they kept coming anyway.

"You won't change your mind?"

Monroe got up and stood between my thighs, gently cupping my face. "No. I won't. Go live your life. Explore and do the things you need to. I'm letting you go because I love you, because I want you to be happy and find a life that suits you. Don't settle in life, not ever. You're too good for that."

I put my hands over his. "And you'll be right here? You promise? You'll always be right here, and I won't have to hunt all over the universe for you?" I whispered.

He leaned in close enough to kiss me on my forehead. "If you come back to this planet, I will be here."

I shook my head and pressed my hands to his chest. "*When* I come back. And I will."

Monroe gave me a little smirk. "That remains to be seen. Take care of yourself, Thierry. Have a good long life. Fall in love with someone who deserves you. Go on adventures and discover new worlds."

I pulled his mouth down to mine and kissed him as hard as I could. I slid my hands down his chest to his stomach and found the button on his pants, but before he would let me get any farther, he closed his hands over mine, stopping me.

"No, we can't," he whispered against my lips.

"One last time," I pleaded with him. He might not have thought I'd ever come back to him, but I knew better. But if he wanted to believe he was done with me, then the least he could do was give me this one last moment between us.

"I could never win with you, not since the first time I saw you standing there with your brother. You looked so scared and helpless."

He let my hands go, and I smiled up at him as I opened his pants enough for me to get my hand inside. He was already hard, as if he was waiting for me. "I *was* scared. Someone had assumed they'd be getting both Corbin and me as a treat one day."

Monroe helped me take off my shirt. "Idiots, the lot of them," Monroe teased.

I laughed as he laid me back and helped me strip off my pants. "Those idiots are your customers," I reminded him. The distinction didn't matter; he kissed me, cutting off anything else I would have said. He was inside of me then, and I let the rest of the world slip away as I wrapped my legs around his hips and focused on only him, and us, and how much I loved him.

Saying good-bye to him that night was the hardest thing I'd ever had to do, and I was still crying when I explained what had happened to Corbin hours later. My brother hugged me and told me it would be okay. I knew it would, that I'd see Monroe again, that he was only a three-minute walk down the main hallway, but none of those facts mattered that night as I lay there, wallowing in misery.

EPILOGUE

I WAS nearly thirty before I set foot on Wish again, and the toils of my youth seemed just a distant memory. The only bright beacon of that time, the only face outside my brother's I still reflected on with seemingly impossible regularity, was that of Monroe. Finding my way back to him had been a long and arduous journey, and one I hadn't been particularly eager to take in the beginning, as it meant leaving him behind. But in all our dealings, we had been businessmen, and I knew if I gave our years apart anything less than my all, he would somehow know and refuse me again.

I was a pilot, a gentleman, and a scholar. I'd discovered whole universes and been right there with exploration teams as the first of my kind to touch new planets. I had done so much to be proud of, and I owed it all to the man inside the office I stood in front of.

I knocked and waited to be allowed to enter. When he called to me, his voice as familiar as it had been the last time I'd heard it over a decade before. I stepped inside a room that had not changed by even a degree in all my time away. Monroe, though, he was older, and his soft black hair was now streaked with gray. He was over fifty now, and the lines around his face showed his age, but that hardly mattered to me.

"I am a man now, and I've done what you wished of me. Will you still deny me a place at your side?" I asked as soon as his gaze caught mine. No other introductions were needed between us. He was as familiar to me as I was to myself. I'd

171

loved him in my youth and even now, with years between our last meeting and this, I still loved him.

"You are a stubborn boy, I'll give you that."

My nervous smile turned into a grin as I saw the mirth in his eyes. "And you are right where you said you'd be. Seems we're both stubborn."

He gave me a little smirk. "Are you so sure you want me now? It has been a long time."

"I am." I was very sure about that.

He got up from his desk, and I waited, so afraid he'd throw me out again, as he'd done the afternoon I'd stood in this very spot a decade before. But he didn't, to my immense relief. A gentle hug between comrades turned into a kiss between friends. And then I knew I had found my way home as his skin touched mine, and I was once again his.

CAITLIN RICCI was fortunate growing up to be surrounded by family and teachers who encouraged her love of reading. She has always been a voracious reader and that love of the written word easily morphed into a passion for writing. If she isn't writing, she can usually be found studying as she works toward her counseling degree. She comes from a military family, and the men and women of the armed forces are close to her heart. She also enjoys gardening, hiking, and horseback riding in the Colorado Rockies where she calls home with her wonderful fiancé and their two dogs. Her belief that there is no one true path to happily ever after runs deeply through all of her stories.

Website: http://www.CaitlinRicci.com

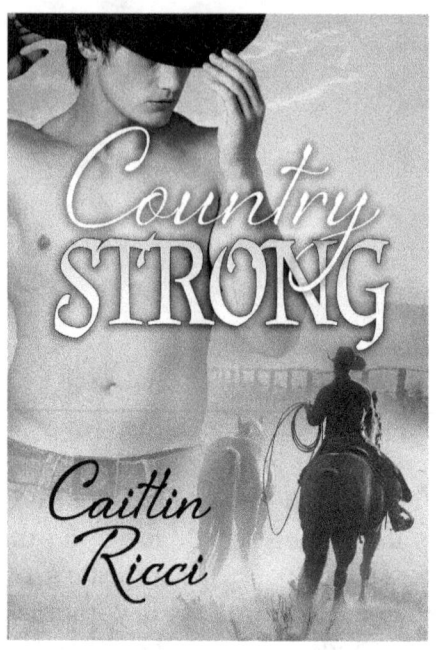

With only three months left on a lease-to-own agreement on a quarter horse Wyatt's worked hard to own, a thunderstorm spooks General and he throws Wyatt, changing both their lives forever. Luckily, Kellen, a friend of the stable owner, calls for emergency medical attention, and Wyatt comes out of the hospital with a broken wrist and a concussion.

When Wyatt returns to the stable, he finds the owner has sold General to Kellen for retraining. But Wyatt's woes have just begun, and now he must drive an hour to see his horse. The perks help balance the hardships, however, and Wyatt finds himself falling for Kellen. His fortitude is soon tested again by the ultimate betrayal when he learns Kellen doesn't intend to return General after he's trained.

http://www.dreamspinnerpress.com

Charlie thinks his Friday will be the same as any other working as an animator, until Quinn Fitzgerald and his rescued Asiatic Lion, Aseem, walk into the studio. While the lion is impressive, his handler is the real reason Charlie's heart skips a beat.

Quinn has devoted years of his life to rescuing big cats, so he can't turn down the donation the animation company is offering in exchange for using one of his cats as a model.

Charlie isn't quite as confident as the handsome, charming man his sister teasingly calls Sex God Quinn Fitzgerald. He's so nervous he can hardly talk to the other man, so he's shocked when Quinn not only notices him but invites him to spend the weekend at his big cat sanctuary.

http://www.dreamspinnerpress.com

Six months after Kit lost his big brother to a drunk driver, he's alone and feeling like everyone has left him behind. He struggles to get out of bed, to feed himself, to talk to his parents. Worst of all, the man he loves, his brother's best friend, hasn't spoken to him since the funeral.

Tattoo artist Jason always planned to wait until Kit was a bit more experienced and mature before he told Kit how he felt about him. But Bear's death changes everything, and Jason opts to give Kit space to heal.

However, the next time they meet, Jason is startled at how far Kit has deteriorated, so he takes him home. Simply taking care of Kit isn't enough. Marking Kit with the tattoo he demands opens a window, but Jason still isn't getting through, until he begins ordering Kit around and sees how receptive Kit is to his strong hand.

http://www.dreamspinnerpress.com

Werewolves are real. Marius enjoys the irony that everyone calls him a dog whisperer, not just because he's a werewolf, but for his work at the local animal shelter. He has a unique talent for pairing families with their perfect pets upon first meeting them. But he's still looking for acceptance and a forever family of his own. Then Jack comes into the rescue looking for a big, mean dog. To prevent Jack from making the wrong choice, Marius convinces him to adopt a needy spaniel mix instead. But when Marius learns Jack is tormented by horrible memories while at his apartment, he opens his home to the sweet, scared man. As their relationship grows, Jack feels comfortable telling Marius about the horrors he suffered. Marius hopes his steady presence, protection, and love can help Jack reclaim the pieces of himself broken on that terrible night.

http://www.dreamspinnerpress.com

SEQUEL TO
RESCUING JACK

A Forever Home
BOOK TWO

OF
Monsters
AND Men
CAITLIN RICCI

Seth's life looks idyllic on the surface. He has a great job at the pet rescue with a fantastic boss, who happens to be a werewolf. He is getting his degree at the local university and has a best friend who understands that the most intimate thing for Seth is a kiss. But when it comes to relationships, Seth's perfect life is a jumbled mess. No guy stays around because eventually, they always want more than Seth, who is asexual, is able to give. Seth wants love and a relationship, but not the sex that everyone puts so much value on.

Seth tries for something more with the man he has a crush on, but when that ends Seth feels like he's back to square one. So when his boss's brother, Jeremy, pushes his way into Seth's life, insisting that he won't press for more than Seth is comfortable sharing, Seth is wary. All of Seth's experience says it won't last long. But Jeremy is one werewolf who is used to getting his way, and might just be patient enough to wait for Seth to see he means what he says.

http://www.dreamspinnerpress.com

http://www.dreamspinnerpress.com

TIME WAITS

C.B. LEWIS

http://www.dreamspinnerpress.com

to be
HUMAN
Pearl Love

REBECCA
COHEN

UNDER GLASS

http://www.dreamspinnerpress.com

EDDIE

SKYLAR JAYE

http://www.dreamspinnerpress.com

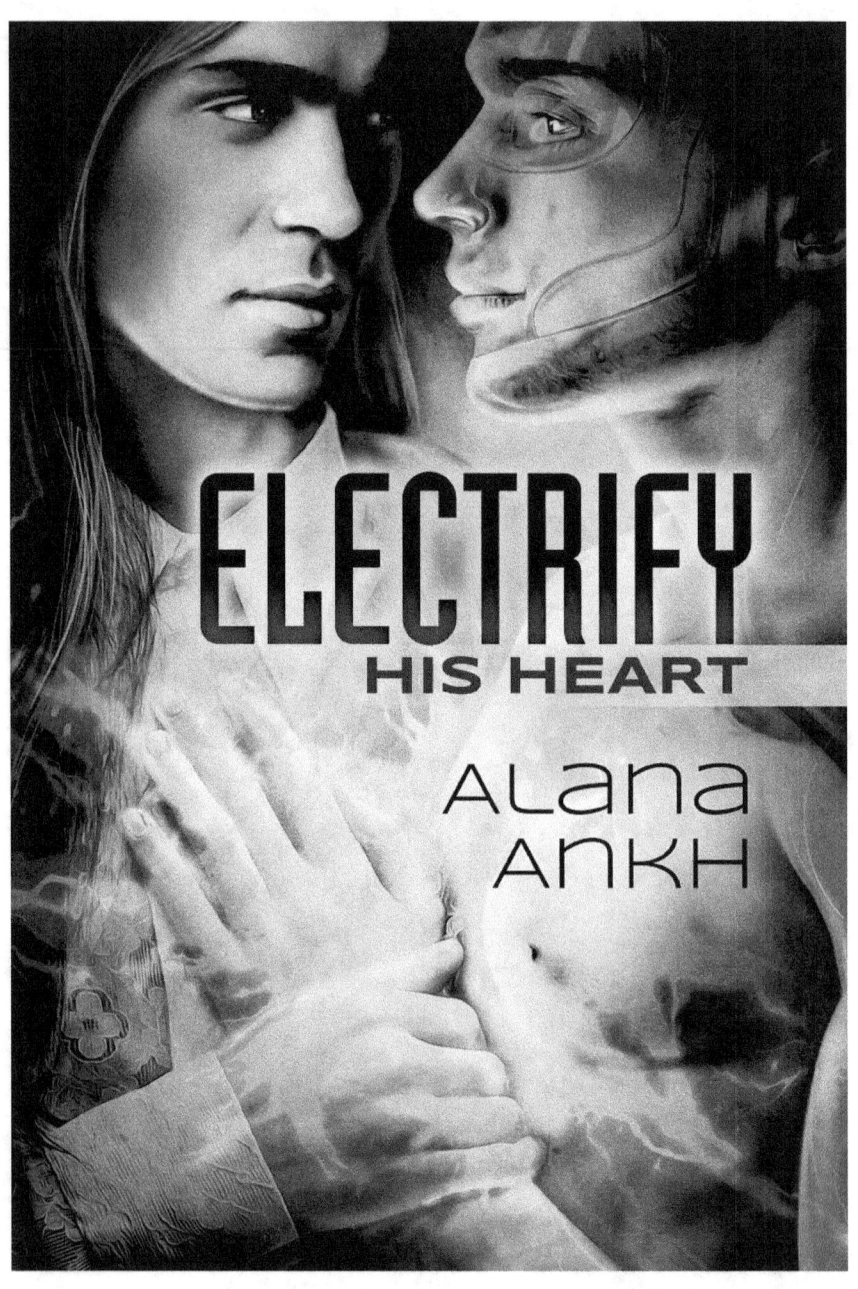

ELECTRIFY
HIS HEART

Alana
Ankh

http://www.dreamspinnerpress.com

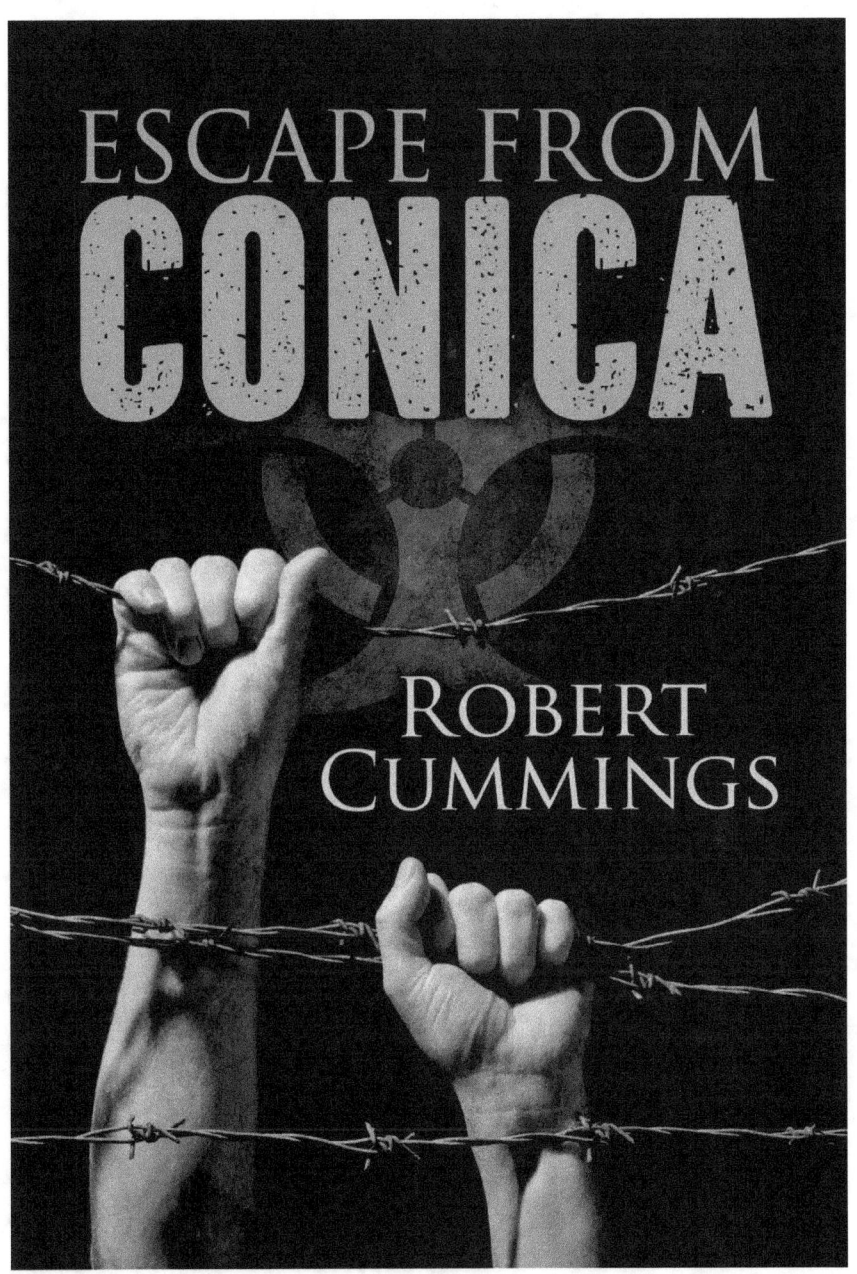

http://www.dreamspinnerpress.com

ALICIA NORDWELL

THE EXPERIMENT

SAVING CAEORLEIA

http://www.dreamspinnerpress.com

GRAVITATIONAL ATTRACTION

ANGEL MARTINEZ

http://www.dreamspinnerpress.com

www.ingramcontent.com/pod-product-compliance
Lightning Source LLC
Chambersburg PA
CBHW060103260626
47160CB00005B/1777